DETECTIVE MACKENZIE
MURPHY SERIES
Cases: 17-32

C.L. CHASE

Chase Dreams Publishing

Detective Mackenzie Murphy Series: Cases 17-32
Published in the United States of America
By Chase Dreams Publishing Fairbanks Alaska

Edited by JoEllen Claypool
Cover designed by Thom Hollis

Chase Dreams Publishing
3875 Geist Rd
STE E, PMB# 149
Fairbanks AK 99709

First printing 2014
LCCN-2014909167
ISBN – 978-0-9904218-2-5

Dedication:

This second book is dedicated to my partner in crime growing up: my brother. We had many adventures and misadventures that was all a part of growing up on a dairy farm. Although there are times where it seems like he has offered no support and only criticism, I know that he is, in fact, one of my biggest fans whether he might acknowledge that or not.

Acknowledgements:

I would like to acknowledge the people who helped make this second book of the Detective Mackenzie Murphy Series a reality. First, a special acknowledgement to my editor and cover designer who really helped put forth time and effort for the book's completion. I would also like to acknowledge my friends, family, and everyone who has a role in the author's life and the author's writings. There have been many characters that have provided the inspiration for the many mysterious characters as both victims and murderers in the travels and exploits of the author. The last thing that requires acknowledgement is the passions and hobbies that have provided inspiration for the various cases that this book contains with cases 17-32 for the reader's enjoyment. Enjoy reading this book.
Compliments of the author:
C. L. Chase

Table of Contents:

CASE 17:
ALASKA AIRPLANE ANTICS

Having rejected going to McCall, Idaho to solve a case, Detective Mackenzie Murphy had rested for a few days before she was requested to solve another case. It was one that would require her to take an airplane flight, like most cases that take place in the great state of Alaska. That was why, on a flight in the forty-ninth state, there were only three passengers, excluding the bush pilot, who was taking them to their destination. The three passengers included a doctor, a lawyer, and a detective. All of the passengers were bound for the same place, a remote village in the northernmost town of Alaska.

The pilot, an experienced old-timer of a bush pilot, made the passengers feel as though they were in capable hands until the aircraft became an object of terror to the people within. The turbulence of the weather outside bounced the plane as though it was a fishing bob in the ocean.

Nothing seemed safer at the moment than the simple every-day tasks of being at home within the confines of a cabin. The bush pilot swore fervently and even vehemently at the weather, at the plane, and even at God at times. Everyone in the plane was on the edge of their seats with clenched jaws in anticipation of what was to happen next.

To make matters worse, solidified dihydrogen monoxide was accumulating on the wings and propellers of the plane. The ice was weighing them down causing them to descend into the unknown below with low visibility to hinder seeing the ground. It was of no surprise that when they came down, they crash-landed onto the ground below with a jolt that made everyone hit their heads on the roof of the plane, rendering all of the plane's occupants unconscious and oblivious to the storm with its snow sweeping across the scenery in its entire sparkling splendor.

When the detective, Detective Mackenzie Murphy came to, it was obvious that the storm was not one to be taken lightly as a mild disturbance, but to be considered dangerous and to proceed outside with caution. Mack, as she was known, knew that it was only a matter of time before the snow would reach the cockpit of the aircraft. With that in mind, she checked the pulse of the pilot only to discover that the pilot was deceased. Checking the doctor and the lawyer, the doctor was the only one who had a pulse besides herself. Knowing this, Mack decided to check the supplies and survival gear. After doing that, she put a blanket on the doctor before she donned her parka and snow pants, vacating the premises.

It was also necessary to walk through the swirling sparkles of snow to assess the situation, with a rope around her waist tied securely to the airplane door. Unfortunately, the assessment of the airplane's condition produced a negative result because there was no way that the plane would fly again without the proper mechanical equipment and parts. A wing of the plane was completely broken off and the engine itself had crashed into a tree. The impact from the crash had caused the engine to be destroyed, forcing it backwards onto the pilot and lawyer.

It was for that reason that the pilot and lawyer didn't survive the impact and if they had, death would have been along shortly to greet them.

Going back to the severed wing that lay cast aside from the actual plane itself, Mack analyzed whether or not the wing could be used as a sled or not. Based upon her observations of the wing's transportation capabilities, Mack fastened a rope to the structure along with the supplies once it had been returned to the general vicinity of the aircraft. Since the doctor was otherwise occupied within a state of unconsciousness, Mack loaded up the doctor, warmly clothed underneath a blanket, onto the makeshift sled. Heading in a northwesterly direction, the long arduous trek towards civilization began.

As the whiteness of the winter sparkled with its entire silvery splendor, the snow just wouldn't end despite looking through sunglasses at the scenery. When conditions turned dangerously close to becoming a blizzard, Mack set up a shelter and all forward progress was brought to a halt in light of the looming weather. That was when the truly unfortunate events occurred to make any rescuers think twice. An avalanche from the mountain above came and covered them in snow. Buried alive beneath the cold snowy surface, it was a fight for survival as Detective Murphy tore her way to the surface. Her next concern was for the supplies and for the doctor who had survived the crash. It was about fifty feet away that the airplane wing protruded from the snow.

Mack ran towards the spot in order to free everything from its firm entrenchment amongst the snow. Once she freed everything, she checked the doctor's pulse and felt a strong steady pulse beneath her fingertips. To her surprise, the doctor was fully conscious and was aware of some of the circumstances leading up to their current predicament.

Thankfully, Detective Mackenzie Murphy had a substantial amount of survival experience and that in itself was the most important aspect of surviving the snowy terrain and solving the problems that were presented by the forty-ninth state in the United States of America.

Setting up a shelter, the two survivors of the plane crash fell asleep, but not before Mack loaded her pistol as a precaution against any unexpected visitors. Slipping into sleep, the snow flashed before the dreamer's eyes as Mack dreamed of her team of dogs and all that lay beyond the boundaries of the current reality.

Officer Tyler Clarke was sitting at his desk at the Fairbanks Police Department station when a ringing phone turned his attention away from his current project. As the papers were left unattended, he dutifully picked up the phone from its pre-determined position on the officer's desk and replied, "Hi, this is Officer Clarke of the Fairbanks Police Department. How may I help you?"

"This is Smiley Sam Smith of the Fairbanks airport. There has been a report that a plane has crashed in route to the northern most town of Alaska. Detective Mackenzie Murphy from the Fairbanks Police Department was presumed to be onboard that aircraft. A rescue team is at the crash site, but there is something that you should know. An avalanche occurred in the area within a five mile radius so even if someone managed to survive the plane crash, there is a good possibility that they wouldn't have survived the avalanche."

"Thank you, but you don't know Detective Murphy like I do. She would never give up without a fight even if there was an avalanche and a plane crash. I've never seen anyone as determined as that detective is. She is the luckiest unlucky person I know and I know that if anyone can make it, that person would be Detective Mackenzie Murphy."

"The chief told me that you were her partner and would at least want to know of these developments."

"Thank you Smiley. Are you at the airport in the event that I need to contact you?"

"Yes, but the chief asked me to have you speak with him before contacting me again. I believe that the chief will be the person contacting me in any case, if the situation calls for it."

"Thanks again."

"You're welcome. I hope that you find your partner. If what you said didn't convince me that Detective Mackenzie was or is one of the best then newspapers and the amount of conviction in your voice would have done it, or the chief would have. Good luck and good-bye." The phone line was disconnected and with it the sound of a dial tone rang in his ears. Officer Clarke hung up the phone. Without any hesitation or distraction to deter him from his course, Officer Clarke went to the Fairbanks chief of police's office and knocked, only to be admitted immediately.

"Have a seat, Officer Clarke. Place your officer's badge on the desk if you will."

"Yes Chief. Might I ask why? My badge is almost as valuable as my gun, at least sentimentally."

"You may ask why and I'll provide an adequate answer to your question in the form of this." The chief said this as he placed a badge in front of Officer Clarke. The officer picked it up.

He took one look at it and said, "This is a detective's badge and I am no detective last I knew."

"Detective Tyler Clarke, you are a detective now and I have an assignment for you. If you are up to it, but if not, then I won't force the issue."

"What is it, Chief? I'm ready for almost anything, I hope."

"I need you to solve Detective Murphy's case. I think that is what Mack would have wanted if she was here and able to make the choice for us. Will you be fine doing that?"

"Yes. You just find Mack during that time. She's good, but she's not that good."

"Don't worry, Detective. We'll find Detective Mackenzie Murphy for you. In the meantime, you will take a flight with Smiley Sam Smith and solve this case."

"Yes Chief. I'll give you an update when we arrive. Let me know if there is anything else that develops regarding Detective Murphy's plane crash and disappearance."

"I will. Talk with you later, Detective Clarke."

"Good-bye." The now Detective Tyler Clarke left for the airport with a pack on his back and a picture of his partner in his pants pocket, safely concealed within the confines of his wallet. It was only a matter of time before

Mack would be found, or so Detective Clarke hoped. Otherwise, he would once again be without a partner and without any hope of having any further partners in his line of work. Setting up another shelter, after the avalanche had wreaked havoc on their previous shelter, Mack had fallen into a deep sleep preventing her from hearing the sound of rescue planes passing. The shelter was an igloo of sorts and wasn't visible by the passing plane due to the fact that all the snow ran together and wouldn't be visible unless the location was known prior to the search.

The world was silent when she woke up from the wonderful sleep and dreams that she had. Looking to where the doctor was, Detective Mackenzie Murphy realized the true extent of the problems that currently faced them. Grabbing a map, she remembered a small arctic village on the way to their case. She made a small calculation of the distance which would bring them to the comforts of civilization and to the crime's vicinity.

Mack prepared food from the gear they had with them while waiting for the doctor to wake up. The combination of the flavorful fragrance of the breakfast, which wafted into the shelter and her own hunger, beckoned the doctor to wake.

The doctor was better from her injuries than Mack had expected since she was able to get around moderately well. As they ate, Mack laid out the plan in all its simplicity and relative ease. Little did they know the challenge that lay ahead of them and time was not to be their friend as it was with the traveling traveler.

A month later. . .

Detective Tyler Clarke had just wrapped up a very challenging case involving a series of bizarre murders. All the murders included seemingly-ordinary objects used as murder weapons such as a tent, yellow igloo cooler top, Dutch oven, flashlight, five gallon water container, and several other ordinary items for a camping experience. The most bizarre event was the fact that the remains of certain anatomy parts were contained in a compost bucket that would have had a sickening smell once summer came. Hidden in the snow, the gruesome discovery never ceased to have its surprises regarding the case. Even with the mystery of the case and all its thought-provoking tendencies, Detective Clarke never fully got Detective Murphy out of his mind. As he loaded his baggage onto the plane, a local Alaskan came to him saying, "Detective, a couple of people just came into town with a hunting party. Come see them before you leave."

"Thank you. I really must be going, but, since you have been so very kind to me, I'll come. Go ahead and lead the way to wherever the hunting party is." Detective Clarke was led to a building that functioned as the city hall and the church. At first, he almost didn't recognize the two travelers until one turned towards him and he literally froze in place, like a statue seeing a ghost.

At least he was until the person came over to him and said, "Tyler, it's good to see you and congratulations on your case. Please take us home with you."

"Mack, you just don't know how to die do you? If I didn't see you for myself then I wouldn't believe it because you're alive and relatively unscathed," Detective Clarke said.

"I know what you mean because it is nice to see you too. Detective work isn't as easy as it appears so good job on your case. Now let's head home since I do believe that a celebration is in order," Mack stated.

"Both of us deserve to go home and celebrate. I can tell you about the case on the flight home if you would like" he assured her.

"We'll have to wait and see. Dr. Price will be joining us and please, just don't have the plane crash. I don't want to have to go insane from insanity and madness," said Mack

"Mack, you're always mad. That's why I call you Mad Mackenzie Murphy." Ignoring that last comment, Mack went over to the doctor to speak to her before they left in the airplane for the Fairbanks airport a short time later.

Two tales were knowledgeably departed to a captive audience of three, holding the audience captivated by confusion. The story of what happened to Detective Murphy and Dr. Price was the first story to be told and it began like this: "Well, you heard that we had a plane wreck then faced the snows of an avalanche, but when we first set off to find the arctic village that our flight had passed, Dr. Price still had to go between walking and being pulled on the airplane wing as I drug our supplies onward. With all the energy I exerted, I had to keep hydrated or I would start having hallucinations. As far as the hallucinations go, I would prefer not to go into detail about that due to the personal nature of the majority of them.

"As the day went on, we were traveling in an area that all we could see was white for miles around and at times, I believed that we were going in circles. There were times that the snow swept all around us so that I could scarcely see my hand in front of my face, but I kept following the compass on a survival knife that had been in the supplies we had brought with us. We went like that for two days, resting at night when the temperature dropped dangerously low. By the morning of the third day, our food ran out despite my efforts to ration out the supplies. Water was our next concern and I kept putting snow in a bottle and warming it with the exertion of my own body just so that I would keep hydrated. I had experienced a worse time with hallucinations during the afternoon than any other day and I made camp that night talking to myself while Dr. Price was sleeping on some blankets.

"I would rather not say what all I said because some things in life just shouldn't be repeated. On the morning of the fourth day, our actual water ran out and it was just by luck that we had managed to make it to the outskirts of the village by the afternoon when I had just about given up on going any further. For a couple of days, we drank only liquids due to our dehydration and the fact that we wouldn't have been able to keep down any solids. After that, we had to wait a little less than a week before we were strong enough to make any attempt at a long trek here with the hunting party. The only reason that I was able to convince the hunting party to take me was because of my expert skills with both steel and lead. Since the doctor was my companion and the fact that I was insistent on not leaving her behind, they allowed me to take her in the sled basket.

"We found game about three days out and we took a day hunting the game before we continued to this village. A couple of hunters turned back with some of the kill as we continued on because they were assured that we would be returned to our own village. About a day longer with the running, my boots gave out on me and my foot got caught on some ice. The whole party had to stop as my foot was looked after and my poor excuse of winter boots were discarded for a pair of these fur-lined boots. When we finally reached the village, I was almost afraid that we had missed the detective assigned to this case and had missed any chance of a ride home. That was why I was really glad when I was able to see such a familiar face amongst this crowd of villagers." It was apparent to Detective Clarke that there was only one component of the Alaskan wilderness that just couldn't be beat and that was the perseverance of its people. It was also a factor that couldn't be forgotten because it was the determined detective: Detective Mackenzie Murphy, the luckiest of the unluckiest who saw the doctor through.

After giving congratulations to the two survivors of the snow, Detective Tyler Clarke began his tale saying, "The case started when I stepped off of the airplane and my luggage fell down into the snow with a crunch. It was as though the snow crunching crunched any confidence confined in my consciousness. A person came up on me as I bent down to recover the bags and I was only able to see some snow boots upon the snow until I was able to come up with the luggage that I retrieved. I met the sheriff, who was just a temporary law enforcement officer to break up fights, but was hardly qualified to solve a murder case of such complexity. We casually acknowledged each other with a nod before we went inside. It was inside the "jail", if it could be called that, that I learned of the case that I was going to be dealing with.

"Outside of town, there was a property with a barn and several structures that held murderous misfits. That is proven by certain discoveries that were provoked by an account of a cry in the middle of the night, providing evidence that they were murderers of a malicious nature. In the woods nearby, a corpse was found dismembered in the snow with a compost bucket about fifty feet away. At first, the bucket had seemed insignificant to me until I found out the reason that it was in such a close proximity to the corpse. Concealed within this container were the remnants of flesh and blood that made a temporary deputy run for the woods with his hand over his mouth, if that gives you any idea of the sickening nature of the scene.

"There was no other qualified person to handle the case except me with my new detective badge and first case to solve. The problematic case stretched out to be a month long because the judicial system set up in the small remote village was inadequate for such a matter. In all areas with the judicial system, people are innocent until proven guilty. Every person who was proven guilty was found to be murdered so that there were only three people from that residence remaining: Zachary Roads, Floyd Ridley, and Lenora Decker. Those three people were arrested and proven guilty of murder. However, the real difficulty of the case was the fact that people still kept getting murdered even with them in custody. It was as though there was a clinically malicious master plan involving a group of people. The criminals were the main cause of the chaos and confusion in the case.

"Only once during the case did any danger present itself with the investigation and it was during an investigation about a person who was murdered by a tent that was closely related to another homicide case that had two murder weapons. The two murder weapons were a flashlight and a Dutch oven and it required the participation of two murderers. It was because of this connection and all of the other connections that led me to an isolated cabin in the middle of some trees. It was upon my arrival that a shot rang out, hitting me in my chest with my bullet-proof vest securely on my body. I was knocked down and I hid behind a tree as I held my gun ready to return fire on the attacker or attackers. As I was ready and waiting for them to try a frontal attack again, I could have been killed from behind. A person had snuck up on me with a club in hand; however, I heard snow crunch with the footsteps in the snow before the assailant went to attack me.

"I intercepted the oncoming club before it could collide with my skull and we wrestled around with the club. We fought with everything we had, ruthlessly trying to out-do the other person, fighting for our lives and freedoms. As we fought, two other people approached and that was when my back-up arrived to help overcome the assailant. The three people, who were there, were the people responsible for the murders and it was once they were in custody that the case was solved. Bringing the necessary answers behind their actions was the fact that they were part of a club known on the internet as the Assassin Acts: a club of assassin maniacs that started taking the game seriously with actual murders." Detective Clarke concluded the conversation about his case.

Shortly after that, they stopped talking and started snoozing from all their exploits of case-solving and survival. As they touched down at the Fairbanks airport, Mack was woke up by a loud cheering crowd. Looking out the window, there was a crowd amassed, holding a sign that said, "Welcome Home". The three occupants saw the support and tears came sweetly shining into their eyes as they looked on. After being gone from Fairbanks for a month, relief was a common feeling among the two dauntless detectives and the solitary survivor of a doctor.

The crowd procured friends and family who took the luggage and hugs of the three people, were now considered heroes, who were on board the plane that touched down. As the excitement wore off, each went their own way to celebrate the fact that they had come home. As for Detective Murphy, she silently stole away to the police department where she made a report to the chief of police who responded by saying, "Detective Murphy, I don't need you here to give me a report on anything today. Go celebrate your partner's recent promotion and your recent survival. I don't need you back to work until Monday unless I call you and say otherwise. Detective Mackenzie Murphy, I offer my congratulations on proving everyone wrong about your death once again. I was just about to write your parents and inform them that all searches had been unsuccessful when I had received Detective Clarke's call."

"Chief, I am no hero and I don't need much rest to be ready to tackle crime. Crime won't rest, Chief. Why does crime take so much time to solve when there are people who are witnesses? I just don't understand people sometimes because of the fact that they are too simple, yet complex. What motivates a person to do what they do and to survive the snow? I may never know, but I tell you what, I am going to try and solve as many complex cases as I can in the hopes that someday criminals might come to understand that they won't get away with any crime they pursue even if they get away with it for a year or more. Do the crime and they'll pay the time."

"Mack, they might never learn, but all you can do is to do the best you can. To do the best you can, you need rest and need to take it easy while you can because if there comes to be a crime spree, you might not get any rest for a while."

"All right, Chief, I'll talk with you later." Detective Murphy left the room, heading to her little cabin that was home and to the hobby of mushing that held her dreams. As the silence and the snow washed over her, Mack knew that dog sledding was the one thing that would never forsake the thrill of survival. It was the one activity that made life interesting and pleasing without all the worry about a detective's demise. Even now, as snow fell from the surface of crystal opaque sky of velvety blackness, the speed of the sled on the snow added a sparkle of light to the detective's eyes. A smile crept onto her features as she forgot all of the events of the past month and only understood the simplicity of the sled and team. Thereby, concluding the case of the airplane antics for the detective and her dreams for the future. As the sunset faded into the horizon, Mack held onto one of the sled dogs in her yard. Feeling the comfort of the furry presence after time spent away from her dogs, it was the perfect end of a day for the detective after a deadly disaster and deathly dealings.

CASE 17 ACTIVITIES

CRITICAL THINKING

In this case, Detective Murphy is involved with a plane crash. What type of things went wrong to cause the crash? How could the crash have been prevented? What would the instruments in the aircraft have read before, during and after the crash? How could have the navigation and knowledge of where they were helped with their rescue? Write down what it might have been like to be involved with the plane crash. What would the passengers' thoughts have been before, during, and after the crash?

REVIEW QUESTIONS:

1) What would it be like to be out in a survival situation? How might you be prepared for a survival situation in the snow? What supplies should you have for a situation like that?

2) What is the significance of the moment where Tyler Clarke is in the chief's office and asked to give up something?

3) How would you feel if you were in the same position that Tyler Clarke was in by solving the case?

4) When was a time that you played a game amongst friends that went bad, even a time when someone's feelings got hurt? How could this example of a personal experience pertain to the case?

VOCABULARY:

Define and use in a sentence based on the definition for the word.

Solidified dihydrogen monoxide-_____

_____

Arduous-_____

_____

Vocab Review: Unscramble the words using the clues given and write down a synonym for the word.

oddiitesren- confused _____

eefabsli- doable _____

lveetnrfy-ardent _____

CASE 18:
CRYSTAL MOUNTAIN MADNESS

Detective Mackenzie Murphy entered into the Fairbanks Police Department with boots and coveralls on instead of the detective uniform that the chief had recently issued. Purposefully, she walked towards the chief of police's office, knocked, entered in and closed the door. Mack was in there for a half an hour before she came out, placing a paper squarely on the chief's desk and then went to her own desk.

Removing everything from her desk, Mack only returned to the chief's office to lay down her badge and gun and to say, "If you need me, I'll be in Idaho with my friends that are actually able to take vacation time without having to quit." She left the room without waiting for a reply from the chief or anyone else for that matter.

After everything was gathered together, she caught a flight to Idaho. Heading to McCall with a couple of friends, they decided to have some fun hiking around that area. Arriving at Crystal Mountain above McCall, they came upon a ceremony taking place. With no time restrictions, they participated in the proceeding. It stretched into the late hours of the night.

When Mack woke up in the morning, the police were surrounding the area. Standing up quickly, Mack lost her footing and almost plummeted down to her death except that she caught herself. Her arms and hands were bleeding on the rock that she clung to with all her strength. That strength seemed ready to fail her when a white wolf-dog appeared on the rocks above her. Feeling a renewed sense of strength, her feet found a strong footing and she felt as though she would live. This thought was confirmed when a person appeared above her at the wolf-dog's side. "There's a person here! Get a rope and pull whoever it is up to take responsibility for their account of the crime."

A rope was lowered and Mack was ordered to place one arm through the already existing loop. Doing as she was told, they pulled her up. The rocks cut her on the way up. It was also on the way towards the top that her head accidentally hit a sharp crystal rock. A person called out for an ambulance and everything went into a deep darkness.

When she woke up, Mack looked around with a perplexed, discombobulated look as she couldn't remember anything of who she was, where she was, or what she was doing there. Looking at a band around her wrist, she realized that her name was Mackenzie L. Murphy. Uncertainty grasped the normally calm and controlled complexion that defined Detective Mackenzie Murphy.

She grasped a bunch of papers and started going through them. The only help the papers were good for was letting her know that she was in a hospital and that she wasn't dreaming because she acquired a paper cut. Placing the papers back down, she heard footsteps coming to her door. Laying her head back down, she pretended to be asleep.

The person who entered into the room started talking saying, "Mack, this is Detective Clarke. I'm not sure that you can hear me, but I wanted you to know that I love you and that I don't believe the accusations against you. Sounds so silly now that I'm hearing it, but it's the truth. I love you Mackenzie Murphy and this case will be solved."

"I'm sure it will be and it is nice to meet you. I don't remember anything. I'm Mackenzie Murphy, right?"

"Mack! You weren't awake just an hour ago, but I decide to make one profound statement and you are awake automatically. Are you suffering from amnesia?"

"If that is not remembering anything then yes, I am."

"I'll be right back, Mack, and don't you dare leave the room." Mack nodded since she had no choice in the matter.

When Detective Clarke returned, there was a doctor accompanying him. Mack instinctively tensed up and the doctor smiled sweetly asking, "You don't remember me, do you?"

"I don't remember anything. Am I supposed to know you?"

"You should because you saved my life once." The doctor replied.

"Well, who are you?"

"Dr. Price and you are Detective Mackenzie Murphy; at least you were. Can you tell me your birthday?"

"No. I don't know what day today is so how should I know what day my birthday is?"

"I don't know, but all we can hope is that your amnesia won't be permanent. We should find that fact out in the next couple days. In the meantime, you'll have to stay here at the hospital to be monitored."

"Mack, I know how much you dislike hospitals so a friendly face will be around to keep you entertained." Detective Clarke assured her.

"Okay." Mack couldn't have said something further from the truth because, at the moment, all she really wanted was solitude and silence.

For the next couple of days, neither of those two desires was answered and more problematic issues were presented. First was the fact that she was the main suspect in a murder that she couldn't remember with injuries that she couldn't remember receiving and a memory that was no memory at all. She had a feeling that she had an experience like this once before, but she just couldn't remember. That was the main problem . . . Mack just couldn't remember.

As the next few days progressed, all that she was able to remember were momentary memories of being shot at, dog sledding, teaching, sunsets with family, and other snapshots into her life before her memory loss. What she did remember, with a frightening intensity, was how much she loathed hospitals.

One day, Detective Clarke was able to take her out of the hospital with an armed police officer guarding her. They went to a location that she recognized and her memory of that area came clearly to her in its entire mental clarity. That led Mack to believe that her memory was on a location-by-location basis and that it was possible that a certain location would trigger the return of a particular memory.

Mentioning this idea to Detective Clarke, they ended up going to McCall with another armed officer to escort them. Crystal Mountain was still closed off for the crime scene. It was there that a scene of dancing came back with the beating of a drum. Suddenly, all movement and sound ceased as Mack sat in a circle with the others in the ceremony. Feeling uncomfortable, Mack had detached from the circle and was walking when she came upon two people arguing. Giving them their space while quietly observing, a glint of metal flashed before her eyes as it was plunged into the person, before being brought down upon the victim once again. The image of the bear drum flashed before her eyes as she realized that she was right there trying to prevent the weapon being plunged repeatedly into the helpless victim. Being hit on the head, she went unconscious and lay still, making the murderer believe that he had hit her in the temple, killing her. However, when she became conscious, she had fallen asleep right there where the attack had taken place.

When the sirens came and the ground gave way, the blood of the victims seemed to make her as guilty as night and day. She remembered the person's name and just hoped that the officers wouldn't think that she was doing the "blame game" by naming another person. There was only one way that she would be able to prove her innocence and that was to find the murder weapon.

As they were looking around the area, two FBI agents appeared out of thin air and arrested Detective Mackenzie Murphy, taking her away from the only friend that she had by her side. All familiarity was a failure and Mack was in the hands of the FBI with their own interrogation techniques. Emotions and thoughts raced through her head as everything was taken from her. She didn't even have her own memories to rely on for what was happening to her.

It was then that she noticed the white wolf-dog looming on the Peak of Crystal Mountain. Already arrested and being led away, Mack decided that she wasn't about to lose her sanity as well. Gritting her teeth, with a determination that rivaled that of a great inventor, Mack broke free from the custody of the FBI. Fleeing into the forest, Mack was truly free upon the forest floor as she ran onward with the FBI in hot pursuit through the forest. The white wolf-dog came in front of Mack and led her to the murder weapon's final resting place. It was there that her memory seemed to come flooding back. Since she knew better than to touch the weapon with her bare hands, the famous Detective Mackenzie Murphy took a nap as she was waiting.

Waking up upon the FBI's arrival, Mack was taken back into custody while the murder weapon was bagged as evidence. Both Detective Murphy and the murder weapon were driven to a secret, undisclosed location under the scrutiny and supervision of the FBI agents. Still, the entire experience was emotionally challenging. Separated from all those friends and family who still cared about her even though her memory had deserted her, she was all alone amongst strangers. It was nerve-wracking to be innocent, while, at the same time, being considered guilty by authorities. The phrase: innocent until proven guilty certainly wasn't in affect here.

Mack was detained in a cell alone in solitary confinement with the cuffs still painfully on her wrists. During that time, Mack pondered escape, but that was all that happened, she never took any action on those ponderings. Using her resources, she acquired a pencil and paper in her cell. Writing and writing, thoughts and words filtered downward onto the page as she was imprisoned. When she was done, a letter was written to Detective Tyler Clarke and Mack carefully folded it, putting it away for safe keeping. The pencil and paper were returned and Mack laid back for a nap.

An FBI agent entered in and woke her up right in the middle of a dream about Alaska. Being taken into a room and blindfolded, Mack outsmarted the FBI because they had no idea how brilliant of an operator she was. Detective Murphy knew the exact location of their facility and she knew the location to which she was being taken.

Thankfully, a friend stood before her and she knew that everything was fine, or at least that is what she thought. It turned out that the familiar person was the murderer and the other FBI agents unknowingly turned her over to the killer. Her friends were both in jail as the murderers and she went with the actual murderer.

They went back to Crystal Mountain and back to the scene of the crime. Bound and gagged, the murderer made a profound statement as a blade flashed forth from a sheath. A knife was in the murderer's hand in mid-motion of being brought down upon Detective Murphy when Mack's hands were freed from the rope bounding her. The knife was blocked en route and a struggle occurred between the captive and the captor. Struggling on the ground, once again, the ground gave way beneath her feet. Mack was able to grasp onto a firm foundation, but the murderer grabbed onto Mack. As she hung there with the merciless murderer's weight dragging her down, she thought that she was dreaming when the white wolf-dog appeared on the hill.

Then a military helicopter appeared out of thin air and freed the murderer from the inevitable fate of death. At the same time, a rope was lowered to Mack. She took it, following instructions, and put it around her arm. Freed from her fate, she was doing great until a crystal rock cracked her cranium and everything went black, but not before a person cried out for an ambulance. For Detective Mackenzie Murphy, it was a déjà vu moment, reminiscent of previous problems.

Waking up in the hospital, Mack was astounded to see a person in a chair waiting by the window. She regained her memory rapidly this time without experiencing the effects of amnesia and memories flooded her mind. She realized that the person in the chair was Detective Tyler Clarke.

While he was still sleeping, Mackenzie went to a phone. The call she made was to the chief of the Fairbanks Police Department in Fairbanks, Alaska. The phone rang for a while before it was actually answered, and even then, it took longer to actually receive the chief on the phone. When he was on the phone, Mack said, "Hey, Chief. This is Mackenzie Murphy and I was wondering if you still needed a good detective for the Fairbanks Police Department or do I have to find another police station to work for that would have me?"

"Detective Murphy, are you ready to come back?"

"If I can come back under my terms and that those terms be acceptable to you and the Fairbanks Police Department."

"Name your terms detective, within reason."

"First, I choose my own cases regardless of the cases and the circumstances. Like the freedom to choose my own uniform that doesn't necessarily give the impression of being an officer, but rather a well-respected detective for instance."

"Okay, go on."

"Also, I want to keep Detective Tyler Clarke as my partner regardless of any personal matters."

"Is that all?"

"Not exactly because I also require the use of a shot gun for cases of dire need. I'm tired of being shot up and shot at and just being shot."

"We'll do better than that Mack. We have a full bullet-proof body suit for you. One more thing, you'll train rookie officers occasionally. Is that a deal?"

"Just so long as I can have a shot gun with my name on it if I need it. Other than that, it's a deal. One other thing, I'll be back in a week if all goes well. I am currently residing in an Idaho hospital."

"Why are you in the hospital, Mack? What happened this time?"

"It's a long story, but I'm sure that you'll hear about it eventually."

"All right, however, I'll expect you in a week and don't get hurt in the meantime. I don't want you to hurt yourself any further, Mack."

"Sounds like a plan, Chief. I'll call you if any problems present themselves."

"Keep in touch, Detective Murphy. I assume that you partner is with you so please let Detective Tyler Clarke know that I want to speak with him when he has a chance." The chief said despite the fact that his thoughts were on the current matter. Although he was somewhat aware of the fact that it had been Matthew Murphy who had called Detective Clarke to Idaho, it was rather surprising that the detective would take personal leave with no other explanation. What was also perplexing was the fact that Detective Clarke had failed to remain in good contact with the chief on the particulars of the matter, but he was sure that he would get the full report with explanation of motives later on. With this in mind, the chief only somewhat heard the response through the receiver.

"I'll be sure to let him know. I'll talk with you later." Mack hung up the phone before she went back to the room. Entering in, she realized that her partner was still sleeping and she hesitated at waking him.

Instead, Mack requisitioned a piece of paper and pen to write down a poem that just came to her. The poem itself was placed where it would be found by Detective Clarke while she went to a mirror. A face as rugged and strong as Alaska stared back at her within the reflective reflections of the surface. If it was so simple to have the marks and scars without the pain, Mack wouldn't be in the horrible hospital. Of all the places to be, she would rather be in Alaska or even at the arctic sea. The temptation to leave from the hospital was unbearable, consuming her every fiber.

As a distraction, she turned towards examining the pictures on the wall. Every detail was taken in. No detail was too small as she examined them all. It was while being consumed by this distraction that she scarcely realized that her partner was awake. She took a double take of the situation to say, "Hi Tyler, I'm glad that my partner's awake. The chief wants to talk with you when you get a chance."

"I'm so glad to see you, Mack. How are you doing?"

"I'm at a hospital, how do you think I'm doing?"

"Maniac Mack is back and this requires some celebration. We can't have a celebration without a present so this is for you." Detective Clarke presented Mackenzie with a necklace that had a crystal rock on it which he offered this explanation: "This came from   Crystal Mountain, but it came in with you so I thought it would be somewhat special to you, at least I hope so."

"Thank you, that's very thoughtful of you."

"I'm glad that you like it. Would you like to go dog sledding with me sometime?"

"Of course, I love dog sledding, but we can't go dog sledding if it isn't in Alaska. It just wouldn't be the same with everything that I've done," Mack informed him.

"That's the truth. I'll get you out of Idaho in a couple of days, but you have to be patient. Also, you will have some visitors in a little while. In the meantime, I'll be out of the room," Detective Clarke explained.

"Thank you and by the way, patient is my middle name as a current hospital patient."

"I know how much you loathe hospitals, but you have people who love and care about you. Just recover for them in the hospital, if not for yourself."

"All right, thank you."

"You're welcome." Detective Clarke left the room.

He returned a few hours later with a surprise. "Hey Mack, I brought you a friend. This is Raspberry and she's yours."

"Thank you. How did you get permission to bring her in here?"

"Actually, I didn't exactly. If anyone asks, I'm a detective and it's all in the line of duty." Mack smiled as she held the amber colored sled dog puppy. It seemed to make everything worthwhile.

It wouldn't be until a couple months later, when the snow fell softly down onto the trail that Detective Mackenzie Murphy would stand upon the runners of the sled. The runners relaxed the detective and she was able to fall asleep at night as she rested her head on the bed. The snowflakes fell softly down, coating the mountains and detective in a white sparkly splendor of dreams.

CASE 18 ACTIVITIES:

CRITICAL THINKING:

In this case, it mentions a Crystal Mountain, which brings us to a question about rocks. What are the different types of rocks? What would a crystal rock be categorized under? Geology is an interesting topic which poses the question: what is the definition of geology? Do some research regarding rocks and write a paper about it. Ask yourself what you would name a rock if you found a new rock that was previously undiscovered?

REVIEW QUESTIONS:

1) What circumstances do you suppose led to Detective Murphy's departure from the police force?

2) What would you have done if you were suffering amnesia that had a complete memory loss? How do you think you would feel?

3) What would be some ways that you could escape from someone that you didn't want to be with? What would you do and think in a situation where you were being held against your will?

4) What arrangements did Mack talk about with the chief regarding her return to the police force? Why would the chief agree or disagree with those requests?

VOCABULARY:

Define and use in a sentence based on the definition for the word.

Plummeted-_____

Acquired-_____

Amnesia-_____

Problematic-_____

Rivaled-_____

Scrutiny-_____

Cranium-_____

Reminiscent-_____

Déjà vu-_____

CASE 19:
SKUZZY SCUTTLE MONKEY

Detective Murphy walked into the Fairbanks Police Department and walked straight to the chief's office. Picking up a badge, gun, and case files, Mackenzie sat down at a desk to examine what she had.

Searching through the files, an interruption occurred when the chief approached her saying, "Mack, we have an officer that will be working with you and Detective Clarke temporarily. His name is Officer Michael Z. Cooley."

"Chief, I just got back from Idaho and you are putting me with a temporary officer?"

"I know, but you are the best so I'm sure that you'll be able to handle it."

"What if I am unable to do so?"

"Then you must not be the best, Mack," the chief shot back.

"I think I got your point, but I feel that I'm obligated to inform you that I can't guarantee that our personalities won't clash to the point that only one of us remains standing."

"Duly noted. Is there anything else?"

"Yes, Chief, am I still able to choose the case we are assigned to?"

"Yes, just choose well, Detective Murphy, that's all anyone can ask. Now, is there anything else?"

"No, Chief, that is everything I believe. At least for the time-being, but I'll let you know if I think of anything else."

"Then you're free to go just so long as you can assure me that you'll do your best."

"I always do, Chief and I'll talk with you later." Mack exited the room.

She was confronted by her temporary co-worker right away with him saying, "Detective Murphy, I'm Officer Cooley and I'm from Los Angeles, California where all the real detectives are from. Fairbanks is in the middle of *#$($ nowhere and I was told that I would be working with you."

"First of all, I don't appreciate that use of such vulgar vernacular language. Secondly, a little bit of humility goes a long way in this part of the world. The only time that vulgar language is acceptable in my line of work is when you get shot, clawed by a grizzly, or other means of physical harm." Mack replied.

"As though you would know, however, I need to go check my hair and see the chief of police of this . . . town."

"That sounds good." Mack let him walk away, all the while thinking of how conceited that officer seemed to be. If he was supposed to be the temporary officer working with her and Detective Tyler Clarke, the chief must be crazy.

Consumed by her thoughts, Mack ran smack-dab into Detective Clarke. Both fell down to the ground and their lips met upon impact, however embarrassing the situation was. Regaining composure instantly, Mack promptly got up with an apology springing instantly to her lips as she spoke the words with a genuine apologetic glance. She then went to find a case worthy of such a logical character that she had and for the people that would be working on the case with her. It was while she was researching the cases that one revealed itself in the form of a command. Detective Clarke and the chief approached her and laid a folder on the detective's desk.

The chief went on to say, "Detective Murphy, I can't force you to take a case on, but this case is our top-priority."

"Let me see it before I consider taking it on." Mack said as she picked up the case file and turned questioningly to the two people who stood before her, saying, "What is this? A cruise ship murder or is it actually a bad movie script that I'm seeing?"

"Not at all Mack, this case is all yours if you want it. It isn't a bad movie, but if Hollywood got their hands on this, it would be."

"I'll take it on because it should be a piece of cake," Mack agreed.

"Thank you Detective Murphy. I knew that I could count on you."

"No problem. Just don't remind me of how much I'm like my father and I'll do a little jig for you."

"Be ready to go in an hour."

"I'm ready to go now. My bags aren't even really unpacked from my vehicle."

"Do you live in your car?"

"Pretty much, at the moment, because I have company at home and the car is the guest bedroom for me."

"In that case, read the file and do some researches while you wait patiently for your partners and let me emphasize the word patiently for you, just so that you'll understand."

"All right, Chief, will do." Mack went to do some research and she pocketed some papers on the information discovered. She carefully kept track of the time. Using her pen and notebook, Mack dutifully jotted down an observation. It was in the bustling office that Mack wanted to escape all the noise and confusion within the department. All the noise reverberated throughout her mind, mentally moving the mountains of mental stability towards madness.

"Mack, you ready?" The question broke through Mack's muses as the instability of her mentality was disrupted.

Looking up, she said, "I'm ready and I've been ready. Is Officer Cooley ready?"

"I'm ready," Officer Cooley said, approaching her with three duffle bags.

"What's this?" Detective Clarke asked.

"It's my clothes. Duh! I can't go anywhere without my clothes because that would be just ridiculously outrageous."

"Officer Cooley, we will be going on a helicopter and not Air Force One for your information. Please have your clothes limited to one bag or you will find yourself left behind at the Fairbanks Police Department."

"Say what? That is just ridiculous, you skuzzy scuttle monkey. Detective Murphy has two duffel bags so why can't I?"

"What? Are you two years old? Just for your information, one of those duffle bags is actually equipment for the case. Just one duffle bag please or you are going to be left here." Detective Clarke casually pulled out a shot gun and started cleaning it, making Officer Cooley cut off his retort and he did what was asked of him. Finally, there was only one duffle for each person and there was another duffle with equipment. It was from the Air Force base near Fairbanks, Alaska that they departed for the cruise ship.

Once on the cruise ship, the real detective work started for the three Fairbanks police officers. Detective Murphy had Detective Clarke and Officer Cooley start interviewing the witnesses, while she saw to the crime scene and to the corpse. It was while analyzing the body that Mack made a discovery about the deed already done. It was in the time shortly after the discovery that Mack's radio clicked on and off three times. Realizing that Detective Clarke was in trouble, Mack went into the large air vents just before someone entered into the room.

Moving caused a noise noticeable by the person in the room and they started firing randomly into the vents while Mack made a hasty retreat deeper into the vents. The assailant radioed to another person as he exited from the room and Mack heard him mention a "Deputy Schneider."

Mack's phone vibrated. Answering it, the hurried voice of her handler came through the line, making Mack ask to have the conversation repeated to which the handler said, "Mack, one of your dogs got loose and we chased her for three or more hours before we finally had to give up. The sheriff's office is aggravated about being called out for a minor disturbance. What should I do?"

"There's nothing that I can do right now. I'm on a case and I need to get off of the phone. Please just handle the situation. I have other things to worry about at this time." Mack hung up the phone, absent-mindedly forgetting to say good-bye, and she realized that one of those random shots actually added insult to injury by inflicting a wound.

It seemed the cruise ship was under the control of a corrupt captain. Mack was the captives' only hope of rescue from the rogue reasoning of the culprits. Detective Murphy then made an exit from the vents into a crawl space when the opportunity presented itself. Mack remembered the papers that she had put in her pocket when she was researching the cruise ship. One of those papers just happened to be the layout of this particular ship and Mack made her way to the dining room where Detective Tyler Clarke and Officer Cooley sat.

It was by observing from a grate that Mack realized the true gravity of the situation. In the middle of the spacious dining area, a deputy was maliciously threatening Officer Cooley with a club in hand and a nefarious smirk on his face as he said, "Officer Cooley, you think that you, as an officer of the law, are above all the small tasks such as seeing to the pooper-scooper duties of the K-9s? Well, you're not. For years, we have dealt with minor nuisances and you think that you are above it? We have had enough of this from the department. This cruise ship has a million dollars' worth of gold in it and we plan to teach everyone a lesson. In fact, it makes perfect sense. We've done our time for small wages in the department and now, we'll do the crime. Now tell me, who is the other person that was with you?"

"You won't get away with this Deputy Schneider. You'll be stopped." Officer Cooley threatened. "I highly doubt that. There was blood in the vent. Your third person is probably deceased as we speak. I just need to know the name to put on the tombstone." Taking a moment away from the conversation to see what was available in the room. What Detective Murphy saw was what any MacGyver would want: military grade C4 that was being shipped to a secure location unknown to any of the guests. Mack got a grin that any kid would have when playing with fire. All that was needed was the all too common luck and lead. Even that was discovered by the detective when she used the supplies she had to create the perfect distraction with darkness befalling the hostage situation.

It was in the darkness that shots rang out and it wasn't until the emergency lighting came on that the fate of the foolish was found. Officer Cooley and Deputy Schneider both lay on the ground and Mack checked Deputy Schneider's pulse only to discover that he was deceased. Coming over to Officer Cooley, it was apparent that he wouldn't make it, but Detective Murphy still called for medical assistance. As Mack knelt by his side, Officer Cooley clutched her arm as he coughed up some blood. With a pale face, he made Mack promise this: "Detective Murphy, you tell my mom and grandparents in person. I haven't done anything good except the police force and even then, I messed that up. Forgive me and promise to tell my relatives yourself."

"I promise, but you aren't going to die. Not on my watch you skuzzy scuttle monkey. Hang in, Officer Cooley, you'll make it."

"Mack, I won't make it and even you know that. Do one last thing for me. Please sing one last song for my ears to hear."

Detective Murphy was taken off guard, but still, she sung the first song that came to her mind which was: "I like to move it, move it."

Officer Cooley's last words before he expelled his final breath were: "Move it." Detective Murphy couldn't believe it and as the medical assistance arrived, she walked like a person in a dream. Detective Clarke came and comforted Mack as they believed the case to be closed. Suddenly, Mack remembered something and she went running to the controls where a co-captain was just coming close to completing a corrupt plan of chaos and confusion for the ship's cruise.

When Detective Murphy entered, she was shot at and went flying back. Getting back up, Mack tackled the co-captain, apprehending him before the plan was fully completed. She received a phone call as she cuffed the co-captain culprit for the confines designated for criminals. Taking the call, Mack said, "This is Detective Mackenzie Murphy speaking."

"Detective Murphy, how is the case coming?"

"Let me call you back, Chief." Mack hung up the phone and took the co-captain to the dining room and handed off the culprit to the control of the other officers who had just arrived as back-up for the case. Being free of the criminal, Detective Murphy returned the call to the chief of police. "Hi chief, this is Detective Mackenzie Murphy."

"Hey, Detective, so how is the case going?"

"Officer Cooley was killed in the line of duty, I took a bullet in my leg, and I used C4 to kill the lights, but I believe that the case is closed. Where does Officer Cooley's mother and grandparents live?"

"According to the records, they live in California. Why? What's up?"

"I'll personally take responsibility for notifying them because of a promise I made. That means that I'm going to California."

"Will Detective Tyler Clarke be accompanying you to California?"

"I'm not sure."

"Well, I have a case for you in California. You can take the case and inform Officer Cooley's relatives at the same time."

"Okay, Chief. I also need to call my dog handler and see about another issue that won't be solved by this closed case."

"Transportation will be along momentarily for both of you and good luck, Detective Murphy."

"Thanks, Chief, I'll talk with you later." Mack hung up the phone before she made the call to her handler. When she heard her handler's voice on the other end, she knew that something was still wrong.

"Hi Mack. We found the dog that went missing, but I couldn't take her back. A family with a couple of kids adopted her and I couldn't bring myself to take her away from them."

"Which dog?" Mack inquired.

"Dokie."

"That's fine. I'm just glad that she found a good home. I'm headed to another case, but I'll be sure to call you before we head home."

"Sounds good, I'll talk with you later Mack."

"Bye." Detective Murphy hung up and they boarded a helicopter once more after she was looked at for her injuries by emergency medical response personnel. That was right before they took the helicopter to an airport in order to board another aircraft, bound for California this time.

Reaching California, Mack and Detective Clarke went to the residence that housed Officer Cooley's relatives. The place was practically a mansion but that didn't seem to faze Detective Murphy like it did Detective Clarke. Knocking at the door, a maid answered and took them to the master and mistress of the mansion. "Ma'am this is Detective Murphy and her partner. Apparently, they worked with an Officer Michael Zachary Cooley."

"Thank you. Please get us some snacks and refreshments."

"Yes Ma'am."

"Please sit down. It's nice to meet you both and how is Officer Cooley doing?" the relative asked of the two detectives.

"That's the reason that we're here. Officer Cooley died in the line of duty here recently and I promised to notify you personally of his passing. He was a good officer and he got his man before he was shot, receiving a fatal injury," Mack explained.

After the initial gush of tears from the grandma, she managed to ask, "Tell me just one thing detective. Was he brave?"

"Yes, Ma'am, he was. He was one of the bravest officers I ever had the opportunity to work with." Suddenly, Mack's phone went off and she had to be excused to answer the call. Once she was out of earshot, she answered the phone saying, "Hello?"

"Is this Detective Murphy?"

"Yes this is Detective Murphy. Who's this?"

"This is an officer from the California State Police. I was told to have you go to the Los Angeles Police Department as soon as possible."

"We'll be right on it. Thank you." Mack ended the phone call and approached Officer Cooley's relatives to say, "I offer my sincerest apologies, but we are needed at the Los Angeles Police Department. Crimes and criminals won't rest for those recovering from a loss. I'll be back later to inform Officer Cooley's mother. Here's my number. Thank you both," Detective Murphy said leaving a business card with her number on it before she and Detective Clarke left the residence and drove to the Los Angeles Police Department. Once they were there, they heard of new developments on the case.

There was someone there to greet them and the officer who met them said, "Detective Murphy and Detective Clarke, it is nice to finally meet you both. We've heard quite a bit of your reputation in Alaska and other places."

"Thank you. I've heard that California was where all the real detectives were. What seems to be the problem with this case at the moment?"

"It is a rather controversial case because it involves minors, drugs, and cold-blooded murder. The suspects are undetermined and our detectives are struggling to find out their identities. Here, this is the case file."

Mack was handed the case file and she looked through it before she said, "This seems elementary and your detectives are struggling with it? May I see the photo enlarged on the computer?"

"Sure, Detective Murphy, have at it."

Mack pulled the image up and said, "This is a name tag on this suspect's backpack. One suspect is Parker Cooley and this is the address. Do I have permission to go pick up the suspect with my partner."

"Certainly, but you'll need these." Car keys passed through the air and were successfully caught by Detective Clarke.

"What do these go to," he asked.

"Click the clicker in the parking lot around our squad cars and you'll find out what it goes to." The two detectives went out to the parking lot without anything else said to the other officer and Detective Clarke clicked the clicker only to see lights flash on a police squad car. It wasn't just any squad car though; it was a sporty classic car with a hemi and new tires on it.

Upon seeing what the key went to, Detective Clarke said, "Mack, pinch me, I must be dreaming."

"Give me those keys, I'm driving." Detective Murphy got the keys and they drove, lights flashing and sirens blaring, to the Cooley's residence. Mack pulled in and saw the suspect fleeing the premises. Stopping and turning off the vehicle, Mack took off in pursuit and tackled him to the ground. While Parker was resisting arrest, he elbowed Mack's nose, causing blood to start flowing. The pain only made her angry enough to punch him and knock him out. Detective Clarke caught up and said, "Mack, you should have been a football player. That was the best tackle and apprehension of a criminal that I've ever seen except for the punch that was probably not in the department's policy. How's your leg doing?"

"The stitches, from the wound that I received from a random shot in the air vents of the cruise ship, opened back up and I didn't even notice or think about it at the time."

"Mack, how mad would you be if I got that tackle on video, but I missed the punching and elbowing because of a low battery."

"We'll talk about that later. We need to get Mr. Cooley into the police vehicle and take him to the Los Angeles Police Department. When he comes to, we'll have to read him his rights." They moved Parker into the back of the police vehicle and Mack tossed Officer Clarke the keys before they headed back to the L.A.P.D. They drove back and it was in the LA Police Department parking lot that Parker became conscious again. It was as though Detective Murphy had planned it because just as soon as Parker was coherent enough to understand them, he was read his Miranda Rights before being taken into the police station.

After questioning Parker, for quite some time, the other suspects were brought in for questioning, closing the case shortly afterwards. Of course, that wasn't taken care of until Parker Cooley had added a charge onto his rap sheet for assault on an officer when he lashed out at

Detective Murphy during the interrogation. Mack received a black-eye and had her wounds attended to by some nurses at the police station.

After the case was closed, Detective Tyler Clarke and Detective Mackenzie Murphy returned to Officer Cooley's residence to see his grandparents again and to meet with the mother of Officer Cooley. It was an emotional meeting and Mack was glad to be done with it especially considering the fact that Officer Cooley's aunt and uncle were also there.

The detectives were also forced to inform the aunt and uncle of the fact that their son was involved with illegal actions involving drug paraphernalia, just to list one of the things for which Parker was arrested.

Needless to say, Mack was all too glad to be headed back home to Alaska and to friends, family, and companions that awaited her there. All Mack saw on the return trip was the back of her eyelids because of the sleep that she experienced: partly because of being tired and partly because of the pain killers she was given.

As she slept, the dreams of snow, sleds, and sled dogs in Alaska came to her as a welcome relief from the fatigue and pain. The dream consumed her in a blizzard of snow, seeking the solace and solitude of the snowflakes as she raced over the snow in search of something special. Something that would mean nothing because that something special would be a day in the life of a detective where there was nothing to solve so that she would be able to sleep softly while thinking of a skuzzy scuttle monkey, whatever that skuzzy scuttle monkey might be.

CASE 19 ACTIVITIES:

CRITICAL THINKING:

What would it be like to be on a cruise? What activities would you do on a cruise? How would a cruise ship navigate and what would it take to run a cruise ship? What would it look like on the ship? Who would you take with you on such a trip? Write a paper regarding what a ship cruise might be like for you.

REVIEW QUESTIONS:

1) How does the temporary partner create stress amongst the two detectives? In what ways does Officer Cooley help with the case and in what ways does he hinder it?

2) How can knowing details about how things work and how things are laid out help someone? How did the knowledge regarding the ship help Detective Murphy?

3) In what ways did the situation on board the cruise ship go right and which ways did the situation go wrong? What would have been some alternative ways to have resolved the situation?

4) Why is it important to keep the promises that you make? How did Detective Murphy keep the promise that she had made to Officer Cooley?

5) What happened at Mack's home during this case that had some sort of significance to the detective? How did it affect Detective Murphy during the case? How would it have affected you if you were in the same situation?

VOCABULARY:

Define and use in a sentence based on the definition for the word.

Vulgar-_____

Vernacular-_____

Paraphernalia-_____

VOCABULARY REVIEW:

Unscramble the word and write down the word's definition.

tlliiiisbea- antonym of assets

_____

Aeerttidlbo- vanquished

_____

mmnneuiaodp- wide spread chaos and confusion

_____

CASE 20:
DEADLY DISASTER

A detective was pacing up and down the room with the footsteps in a precise and methodical rhythm. Another person's life was hanging in the balance in the other room due to a situation provoked by another individual's appearance. There was another person in the waiting room who handed the detective a coffee cup with a note written on it that said: "Don't worry, it's in the hands of a greater authority than all comprehension." The detective was somewhat reassured by the note, but his mind kept coming back to the closed case.

The case started off on a cold chilly day beginning with a cold-blooded catastrophe. A family was found murdered in their own business and placed in a freezer. It sent chills up the detective's spine just thinking about it. Ironically enough, the business was called the Igloo Inn.

The most disturbing fact of the case was that the family pet was also murdered and frozen in the freezer. As disturbing as that was, the detective in charge of the investigation was undisrupted as she coolly analyzed the crime scene as though it was a painting in a museum that needed to be studied and meticulously examined. That was when Detective Mackenzie Murphy discovered a frozen fingerprint on the corpse with a part of the skin suspended there, waiting to be found. Enough of the skin was left for a sample and that was tagged as evidence to find out who the killer was. That was when all the trouble really started because Detective Clarke went to put away the evidence and someone locked the freezer door.

Trapped behind the thick metal door, Mack had to act quickly. Searching through her pockets, Detective Murphy clutched a knife in her gloved hand as she opened a grating to the cooling unit. Inside the grating, she found a homemade detonation device with fifteen seconds remaining. It was all that Mack could do to take adequate shelter from the blast that was going to come.

When the explosion hit, the door shook on its hinges, but remained locked. A swarm of people were on the scene and Detective Clarke had the door unlocked to see the devastation that had been done. Only a person with malicious intentions would think of doing of such a deed. Surveying the damage, Detective Clarke couldn't see his partner, the famous detective who always had a knack of beating death no matter what situation she was in. To Detective Clarke, it seemed as though the detonation was devastating, resulting in a detective's demise. Then a pile of rubble moved to reveal Detective Mackenzie Murphy, mad and muddy, or rather dirty, from the memory.

Mack went on to say, "That is the last time that I go anywhere without my detonation for dummies booklet. Whoever is responsible for this wants to question my intelligence by being one step ahead of me to make me out as a fool. I have a newsflash for them because they aren't perfect and they are reckless, leaving clues and evidence in their haste."

"Mack, you do realize that you have a cut on your eyebrow? There's blood all around your eye. Let's get that taken care of before you go on with your famous Detective Mackenzie Murphy Madness."

"Oh, I hadn't really noticed so just put some duct tape on it and get on with the case."

"Easy Mack since you just about got blown up. Don't let your wound get infected. Take a couple of minutes for yourself."

"Okay," she agreed.

Just then, the radio came on with the chief's voice saying, "Detective Murphy, there has been another murder that you should attend to. Write down this address that I give you."

"Okay, Chief." Mack wrote down the address as she quickly shot an "I told you so" look at Detective Clarke, proving that she was right once again. They went to the crime location only to see a familiar scene because of the fact that it was very much like the one they had just come from only that the corpses were spread throughout the house in cooling units: an ice chest, a refrigerator, and coolers. That was when Mackenzie made a connection between the killer and the victims so she asked, "Tyler, do you have any idea of who the culprit is yet?"

"No. Why?"

"I'm just asking because there were five families that advocated the expulsion of a student whose father was an ice-fisherman during the winter and a commercial fisherman during the summer. The father also has military experience and a very nasty temper when there's anything that regards him or his family. I watched the entire ordeal and I believe that he is my most-likely guess regarding a culprit at the moment."

"How do you know this?"

"I like to keep up-to-date on all the court cases and the fact that I was on the jury of sorts that was formed during the inquiry. It was one of the times that the education board certainly felt like a jury if it wasn't actually able to be considered one at the time."

Suddenly, an officer came up to the partners and said, "Excuse me, but the chief would like to talk with you Detective Murphy."

"Thank you. I'll be right there." Mack got on the radio saying, "This is Detective Murphy speaking."

"Mack, I want you off this case."

"What? Why? I never start a case that I can't finish," she argued.

"I know that Detective Murphy, but your suspect is out for blood and according to the lab results and the suspect's profile, it seems like you are one of the people who will be targeted. I don't want you to die on me just yet so you're off the case."

"All right, Chief." Mack said grudgingly.

"There's one other thing Mack."

"What's that?"

"Tell Detective Clarke that he's on the case. In the meantime, Mackenzie, I want you to get yourself some rest. Can you manage that?"

"Yes, Chief, I believe that I can," Mack said before she got off the radio and went up to her partner to say, "Tyler, you're on the case and I'm off by no choice of my own. That was the chief's orders along with ordering me to get some rest."

"Then I'll see you later, Mack, and be sure to do as the chief says."

"Sounds like a plan. I'll see you later." Mack left the area in her own vehicle and, rather than going home, she went to the family's residence that was in jeopardy and knocked at the door. It was answered immediately and she explained the circumstances behind her visit. They admitted her into their household and Mack entered in with a duffle bag before she closed the door behind her. Once inside, she said, "Now that I've explained the situation, I believe that it would be wise for you to hide in your underground basement. I promise to defend you with my life if need be."

"Okay, Detective. Thanks," they said as they consented, taking emergency supplies with them. Fifteen minutes passed before the fisherman entered into the building only to be confronted by Detective Mackenzie Murphy. He had a weapon out, meeting the barrel of Mack's shot gun and with guns pointed at each other.

The man finally said, "I figured you'd get in my way, but this family got my son expelled."

"No, you are mistaken in this matter. It wasn't the families you murdered or the families that you are trying to murder who got your son expelled. It was me. They had no say in the final judgment call. I did. They aren't to blame so, if you are going to blame anyone, blame me. Your son also needed a certain amount of accountability and is to blame for his own actions that resulted in the expulsion, but not you. Why are you doing this?"

"I believe that they were wrong because my son isn't a kid worthy of expulsion."

"Actually, you're wrong about that because I have had your kid in my class and he did reap what he sowed so to speak." Just then, the door opened in the front of the house and two shots rang out followed by officers swarming the scene. Detective Clarke entered in and his first concern was his partner lying on the floor with blood trickling from a wound in her chest or lower left shoulder. It was hard to determine where exactly the bullet had hit; however, he came up to Detective Murphy who whispered, "Thanks. The family is safe in the underground basement of the house."

"Easy Mack, you'll be all right. Get that ambulance on its way! How's the other person doing?"

"Just a shoulder wound and not too serious of a wound at that, Detective Clarke," shouted another officer.

"Okay, get him in cuffs and we'll take him to the hospital. Somebody keep pressure on Detective Murphy's wound and I'll be right back." Detective Clarke went to the basement, informing the family that the immediate threat was over. When he returned to his partner, the ambulance had just arrived on the scene with its sirens and flashing lights. It was an intense moment as Detective Clarke saw his partner Detective Mackenzie Murphy carted away, leaving him to follow in a squad car. Once there, Detective Clarke was in his current predicament of waiting for news, any news, on Mack's current condition.

A doctor finally came out to tell the waiting friends the news of their friend and/or co-worker. Right from the first moment that he saw the doctor, Detective Clarke realized that there was bad news, but he didn't know exactly how bad it was until the doctor said, "I regret to inform you that due to unforeseen complications that arose, Ms. Mackenzie Lynn Murphy didn't make it. I'm truly sorry for all of you and I offer all my condolences to each and every one of you. We tried to the best of our abilities, but sometimes, these things happen and there is nothing that we can do. Sorry."

"No, this can't be," Detective Clarke said as he walked out of the room followed by another officer. He went to a restroom and locked himself inside its white walls as he tried to grasp the extent of his sorrow. He ended up sitting there crying and sobbing, terrified at his own show of emotions. It seemed to be about a half an hour later that he washed his face of the tears, calming himself of his emotions at the same time. Exiting the restroom, Detective Clarke saw the Fairbanks Police Department's chief of police waiting for him.

He said, "There you are, Detective Clarke. I was beginning to worry about you in there."

"Thanks, Chief, but I quit. I can't do this anymore knowing that Mack's dead," Detective Clarke said as he relinquished his badge to the chief.

"Tyler, I have a proposition for you. Take two weeks and think about your decision. Right now, you're in an emotional state that isn't the best condition to be making any decisions. On that note, I'll have someone drive you home since you are in no shape to do so."

"Thanks, Chief."

"Detective Clarke, there is one more thing. First of all, here's your badge back, I think that you'll need it for your decision."

"What's the other thing?"

"Detective Murphy's funeral should be in a week and I'll let you know all the details. I'll have someone drop off your vehicle and if you need anything, give me a call."

"Okay. Thanks, Chief. Just get me home so I can handle my grief in peace." Without anything else to say, Detective Clarke walked with the escort provided as he was taken home. Once at his home, Tyler finally gave into his grief before he fell into a restless sleep with dreams of his partner, Detective Mackenzie Murphy.

One Week Later. . .

Detective Clarke washed his face and put on his black suit with a black shirt and tie that represented the grief within him. For some strange reason, possibly out of habit, he took his gun with him although he hardly noticed because it seemed natural to take his gun wherever he went. Putting a handkerchief in his pocket and grabbing his wallet, a honking horn of a car broke through the moment of silence. He went out the door, getting into the car that belonged to his family. Once he got in and was seat belted, he said, "Thanks, Dad."

"You're welcome, Tyler. It's the least we could do, all things considered. Detective Murphy was your partner and a hero, bringing you home alive after every case. I'm sure that Detective Mackenzie Murphy will be sorely missed by the entire Fairbanks Police Department."

For the rest of the drive, there was nothing but the symphony of solitude and silence as though the entire world felt the loneliness of loss. It was a lovely funeral for the most part until a person pulled out a pistol and fired into the casket. When the person was forced to reload, the door of the casket came open. Inside the casket, there was nothing, not really enough room for a body, that is until the bottom opened and Mack pulled out a tranquilizer gun. Firing a shot before she ducked back down, the shooter was neutralized and sedated by the tranquilizer.

Detective Mackenzie Lynn Murphy got out of the casket and looked at the crowd amassed before her. Speaking to the crowd, she said, "Thank you all for coming. It was really a lovely funeral with everything that I wanted. Good thing that no one spoke ill of the dead." Mack said jokingly before she said, "On a more serious note, I apologize for the deception. However, it was necessary to ensure that I wouldn't actually be dead. Thank you all for coming and I'll see you later."

Without anything more that could be said on the matter, Mack got into a vehicle, leaving while everyone was slack-jawed, shocked, and flabbergasted at what had just happened. Tyler Clarke got a ride from his family to the police station where he was dropped off as they headed home. As he approached the chief's door, he heard Detective Murphy talking within the confines of the chief's room. Tyler knocked at the door before he entered in without waiting for a response from the chief. Both occupants looked at him as he entered and shut the door.

"Did you know about this, Chief?" he inquired.

"Yes. Detective Murphy was worried about compromising another case by having a criminal after her. It was her idea about the funeral, although I did agree to take part in this plan of hers."

"This was a case of Mack's madness in motion, but why wasn't I told of this arrangement?"

"I felt as if you didn't need to know. If it's any consolation, you were mentioned on the list," the chief defended.

"Easy you two, it is elementary for a detective to deduce the dutiful demise. If you don't mind, I have already attended my own funeral in the casket and I'd really like to get some sleep. Of course, that'll be after I know that my partner has my back. Tyler, are you going to stay away from the police force or will you be coming back?"

"Chief, I'll be keeping this badge since my partner has returned from the "dead" and Mack, I'll take you home."

"Thanks." They left the chief's office and Detective Clarke took his partner back home to her cabin.

Once they were at Detective Murphy's residence, Detective Clarke followed her inside the house and said, "Mackenzie Lynn Murphy, when you died, I felt as though I had lost my best friend after two years. Hear me out about this: I don't ever want to lose you again." Detective Tyler Clarke dropped down onto one knee and asked, "Mackenzie Lynn Murphy, will you marry me?"

"Tyler, I wish that I could give you a definite "yes" or "no", but I just can't at this time. I have so much to…"

"Don't worry Mack; I'll wait for your answer because you are worth waiting for."

"Thank you." Tyler left Mackenzie's house a little disappointed, but hardly discouraged.

Mack pulled out her cases right by the recliner. She curled up in the recliner disappointed at herself for not giving her partner a definite answer. Despite all the tension that she had, she still managed to relax enough to fall asleep. As she dreamed, there was a dream of the snow falling softly from a dark Alaskan sky. The aurora borealis showed up and danced across the dark sky as the sleeping sleeper slept. As she dreamed, dog sled runners crunched across the snow as it was pulled by a team of six dogs.

As they ran, the dogs' tongues hung out of their mouths with happy pleasure as they gleefully plunged forward in their harnesses. They fell into a sense of rhythm as the gang line fell up and down as it was kept taut by the lead dogs. Even as the sled slid onward, it dissipated into a swirl of snow as the dream came and fleeted from the complete relaxing sleep with no dreams to disrupt the sleep's deepness. No one would have thought of the events that happened to call such a case: a deadly disaster. Only the detective sleeping in the recliner could have proved the point that the only deadly disaster was the deceit that had been behind the case of the Deadly Disaster.

CASE 20 ACTIVITIES:

CRITICAL THINKING:

In this case, the motive of the suspect was the direct result of the expulsion of a student by the school board. What exactly is the purpose of the school board? How do they help or hinder student's progress? What would it be like to be on the school board? Who do you think would be on the school board? Write a paragraph or two on your findings regarding school boards.

REVIEW QUESTIONS:

1) What was the suspect's profession? How did this play a role in the criminal acts that person committed?

2) Why did the chief pull Detective Murphy off of the case? Why do you think he put Detective Clarke on the case instead?

3) Based on your own thoughts, why did Mack decide to disobey the chief's orders for rest and helped a family who was targeted by the murderer instead? Would you have done the same or would you have rested at home?

4) Name two significant events happened regarding Detective Clarke after Detective Murphy was pronounced dead by the doctor?

VOCABULARY:

Define and use in a sentence based on the definition for the word.

Expulsion-

Condolences-

Advocated-

Malicious-

Jeopardy-

Relinquished-

CASE 21:
THE MERCY MURDERS

Snowflakes fell from the velvety night sky in silence as Christmas lights decorated the town in the night's reflective radiance. The truth be told, it was a sight to behold. With Christmas just two weeks away, Santa Clause could make any child's day with pictures of Rudolph, the snowmen, and snowflakes sweeping the sparkling scene.

Despite all the decorations and cheer from the season, Detective Mackenzie Murphy was hard at work trying to find a case interesting enough within logical reason. It was then that the detective made a uniquely intriguing discovery. There were three cases of children with ailments of an unhopeful nature at a hospital visited by a Santa Clause. The only problem was the anonymousness of the Santa Clause in question. Even stranger still was the fact that there were four related cases that weren't visited by a Santa Clause character, but were all somehow connected by the means of the murders were acts of mercy in which the victims were essentially put to sleep. It was as though murder was an act of mercy rather than the mentality of madness which it actually was. For some reason, Mack realized a detail in the other cases considered irrelevant by the other officers.

That detail that had been taken into account by Detective Murphy was the amount of money found in the victim's pockets. No child would have had seventy dollars in their pocket and that was evidence towards the fact that the murderer had mercy towards the victim and their family. Upon this discovery, Detective Mackenzie Murphy picked up the case files and took them to the chief of police as he was sitting at his desk. It was then that she said, "Chief, I found what I can work on for a while until Christmas comes to town."

"Mack, what project did you find now?" the chief asked as Detective Murphy put the files down on the desk. He picked up the case files and reviewed them then asked, "Mack don't you ever rest?"

"Does crime ever rest, Chief?"

"No, but you didn't answer my question."

"To answer your question, I believe that I did rest, Chief. Now can I have the case or can't I?"

"Mack, you do realize that I'm still receiving requests for your services right? There's one case that seems to be perfect for you in Canada according to what I've heard."

"What's it about?"

"It's about a farmhouse murder where the culprit got away on a horse-drawn sleigh."

"Chief, I would much rather solve this case, but you can put Detective Clarke on the Canada case."

"All right, that should work. It might provide both of you the opportunity to value your partnership," the chief remarked.

"That's the reason that I'm recommending to be on different cases."

"Your point is taken. Just get on with the task that you are so impatient to be working on right now."

"Thanks, chief, you're the best."

It was as Detective Murphy was just about ready to leave that an officer rushed into the chief's office saying, "Chief, there's been an incident in Nome where a famous actor was found dead in their hotel room. They're requesting that you send your best detective to aid in the investigation."

"Mack, I need you on this new case because the other case is simple enough that someone else can handle it."

"All right, Chief, I'll take the Canada case."

"Detective Murphy, you are going to Nome and that's final. Okay?"

"I guess that I don't have a choice in the matter or do I?"

"No, at this point, I want you to be on the Nome case with Detective Clarke."

"Fine, when will I be going?"

"You won't be going anywhere Detective Murphy and neither shall you, Chief." This was said after the officer had left the room by a person who was hiding in the office. It was with a cleverly concealed key from a family friend who had worked for the police department's holding cell that he had managed to escape. With the man present, the chief was shocked at the prospect of being held at gun point in his own office.

"What's this about? We haven't done anything to you have we?" the chief inquired.

"Actually, unless you include bumbling incompetence as a cause for wrong doing then no, you have not. I have a case for you. A case that will prove my innocence for a crime that I was convicted of."

Mack picked up the case and flipped through it before saying, "You're right about your innocence, David Thomason. The only question is who actually committed the crime if you didn't and can we find the culprit? Chief, may I be on the case?"

The chief sat staring at the black barrel of the pistol as though it marked his impending doom before he managed to say, "Yes Mack you may. I don't think that we have any choice in the matter to do otherwise. We'll send someone else to take care of the case regarding the actor in Nome, the case of the horse drawn sleigh, and whatever other case you had. Take your partner with you and whatever you do, solve this case." The chief said this to clarify the case that Mack was supposed to be working on due to the fact that there were three or four cases originally presented for the two detectives.

"I will. David, if you're innocent, which I believe you are, will you hand over the weapon? Please?"

"Yes of course." The man said handing over the weapon willingly.

"Thank you. You have my word that I'll solve this case and if you don't believe my word is good enough then you obviously don't know me."

"I'm no murderer and I'll trust your word that you'll prove that."

Mack left the room and went to her partner and said in an authoritative voice, "Detective Clarke, get your feet off of the desk and put that dreadful donut down because we've got ourselves a case to solve."

"What is it this time? Did some kid's dog eat his homework?"

"No. Why would we be investigating that?"

"Never mind, so what's the case?" Detective Clarke asked intrigued as to the case.

"Here, have a look at it, but here's the overview: someone shot down a Santa just recently and they pinned it on this man: David Thomason. It was a crowded mall yet with all the people, the cops that were on the case made a hasty search and arrested Mr. Thomason. What does that tell you about the case?"

"They were dirty cops or at least cops that didn't care either way just so long as they had the case solved."

"Now you get it, but there is something else that will work to our advantage."

"What's that?"

"The mall security held on to the security footage so if we could figure out the killer by the footage then we will have our culprit to take into custody. I guess that we'll have to go shopping for a suspect."

"What's the plan?" Detective Murphy got one of her mischievous smiles just before she told him the plan while they were headed to the Fairbanks municipal mall. Once they got there, Mack went to the scene of the crime while Detective Tyler Clarke went to see the security footage. Mack analyzed the angles that a shooter could have positioned him or herself, knowing full well that the body and pictures all had a story to tell regarding the crime.

Once they were back to the station, Detective Murphy was analyzing the footage and the angles, pursuing all of the possibilities. Breaking through her thoughts was the voice of Tyler as he asked, "Mack why are you so silent?"

"I'm thinking which means that when I'm in the zone, leave me alone."

"Fine, I'll go get us some coffee. We've been at it for four hours and it seems that I have been staring at one screen or another for too long." Detective Clarke went off as Mack was still overcome by the maddening fact of the murderer's madness. Creating the scene of the crime and the stores in the mall, she realized that one of those stores just happened to be the Salvation Army and that was when she made a connection between the current case and several other cases.

After reviewing the tapes, her suspicions were confirmed and, forgetting all about the coffee that Detective Clarke was off getting, Detective Murphy went straight to the chief's office. As she entered after knocking, the chief said, "Detective Murphy, what have you found?"

"This case is connected to the other cases that I had mentioned earlier."

"What cases were those?"

"Those were the cases that I first mentioned about the Santa Clause and the nun and the mercy murders. The victim in this current case was terminally-ill from cancer. All the killings were merciful, meant to not prolong the suffering. It was as though they were killers or assassins with hearts of gold."

"You don't seriously believe that, do you Detective Murphy?"

"Chief, I believe in justice and what I believe or feel is irrelevant in the due course of the law. No matter what the circumstance or how merciful murder may seem, there is still justice to be served regardless of what I may believe to be right or wrong. Even right or wrong seem a little fuzzy at times. The only thing we know for sure is that a person must accept the consequences of their actions no matter the price."

"When will the case be solved?" The wrongly accused man asked her.

"I'm not sure because I have to compile the evidence and then get the culprit's confession. I expect it to be just a day or so."

"What do you suggest?" he asked.

"I suggest that we take you into custody."

"But. . ."

"Hear me out on this because I have a plan. First of all, you'll be fed and taken care of while you wait and as an added bonus, you'll have more protection than you would otherwise. Things have a tendency of getting a little violent around here and I want to make sure that you don't die for a crime that you didn't commit."

"Thank you, Detective Murphy."

"You can thank me after the case is finished and not before then. I'll let you know if I catch the killer or if there is anything else that you need to know." Detective Murphy walked out of the room without saying anything else to either of them on the matter.

After she had left the room, David Thomason asked the chief, "Does she do that often? Just walk out of here without saying a word with a determined look on her face as though she is going to cure the world of hunger?"

"All the time and after a while, you just have to get use to all that Detective Murphy does. Even if I question some of the things that she does, she always solves the case when I think that no detective ever could," the chief said with a distant look as he remembered all the cases that Detective Murphy had been doing for their department and others.

Mack returned to the room that she had been working in and found Detective Clarke waiting on her as he was sipping his coffee. The moment that she walked in the room, Tyler asked, "What'd you find out?"

"This case is connected to another string of cases that I noticed earlier today." Suddenly, the computer started flashing with a match found as the current culprit was identified by the computer's analyzing system.

When the match appeared on the computer screen, Detective Clarke said, "Mack, I've seen this person before."

"So have I. He and his wife have been to the police station when their son, Johnathan, was missing. John, as he was known, had cancer and he ended up being found dead after he had taken his own life, leaving only a suicide note for his parents and family," Mack remembered.

"I remember that and things are finally making sense. All we need now is a signed warrant from a judge to be able to arrest them and take them into custody."

"You get that while I wrap up all the evidence for the case right here. There just a few things that need tending to."

"Sounds good, Mack and I'll give you a call once I have the warrant." Mack nodded as she went back to the daunting task of organization and paper work.

It was as she was ordering the cases in chronological order that she noticed something intriguing. The first letter of the victims' names spelt out J-O-H-N-A-T-H-A-N. It was then that she made the connection as she realized that her first and last names both started with an "M", the middle initial of John's name. She put the files up after trying to think of who the couple's next victim might be. Mack had just holstered her pistol and grabbed her radio when she heard the resounding click of the hammer being drawn back to fire if necessary. Ever-so-slowly, Mack turned around to face her attacker only to see Santa Clause and a nun both pointing a pistol at her. With a self-satisfied smirk, the nun said, "Well, if it's not the famous Detective Mackenzie Murphy."

"Very clever by the way, using your revenge to spell out your son's name, but I thought that your victims were all suffering from a deteriorating state and I'm not currently experiencing such a state of unhealthiness."

"We decided to make an exception, at least in your case because of your apparent ill mental health."

"Very interesting, but I just have one question."

"No, you don't because you are coming with us right now." They moved Detective Murphy to a different area after blind-folding her. When they finally arrived at their destination, they were at a place on the outskirts of Fairbanks. She was taken out of the vehicle and rushed into the house before the blindfold was taken off. Directed by a pistol, Detective Murphy was placed into a confined space below a throw rug. It seemed to be a cellar, but the pipes proved that the space was actually beneath the house.

It was there that Mackenzie was able to find two different means of escape and she took one of them. Once out of the house, Mack hid in a dog house nearby, knowing that they'd check the shed first, not suspecting that the detective would be going to the dogs. For some strange reason, unknown to her, the couple that was holding her hostage didn't body search her so that she still had her gun and radio. Mack also had her cuffs on her person, ready and waiting for instances like these. When both of the criminals realized that their prisoner had escaped from one point of weakness, the shed looked like a safe place to check for the escapee just as Detective Mackenzie Murphy had expected they would.

Waiting for that moment, Mack got out of the dog house and whacked one over the head with the pistol when a shot was fired followed by a second retort that was lower than the first as the second culprit was royally conked over the head by the pistol. Shortly after the shots were fired, a man came busting over a yard gate with a pistol in hand, yelling, "Freeze!" Mack froze with hands raised before saying, "I'm Detective Mackenzie Murphy and I've apprehended two suspects. I take it that you must be an undercover cop for the department?"

"Yes, I am, and I was investigating a disturbance in the area. I heard the shots and my partner radioed in that there were shots fired at this location. Is anyone hurt or did those shots just hit dirt without coming into contact with anyone?"

"One shot hit the wall behind me and the other managed to make contact with flesh. It's just a leg wound, but could you put these two in your squad car? I'm sure that back-up will arrive here in a minute or two so that I can get help, at least for my leg wound, that is."

"You're mad aren't you?"

"Detective Mackenzie Murphy is always crazy, but, thankfully for you, you don't have to get use to the lunacy. Thank you, Officer, I'll take care of Detective Murphy from here," Detective Clarke's voice answered.

"How'd you find me? Did you listen to the police scanners?"

"I was on my way to the judge's place to get a warrant when I was told the residence that I knew to be the suspect's place. I came only to find out that it was and that my partner was already here. I guess that I didn't need that warrant anyways. It looks like you managed to get injured again, so let's go take care of that leg."

"Good idea and I know a clinic not far from here that would fit the bill figuratively and literally speaking. In fact, I'll drive there so I don't have to instruct you."

"You'll do no such thing. I'm driving," Detective Clarke argued.

"It's just a leg wound so I can still drive."

"It's my vehicle, my keys, so I'll be the one driving. Come on Mack, it's not like it'll kill you to let me drive."

"You don't actually want me to answer that do you? Probably not so I guess that I have no choice in the matter. By the way, you do know that payback is possible and highly likely?"

"Sure, sure, let's just go because that wound isn't healing itself."

"I'm coming." They drove to a nearby clinic once they were both securely fastened into the vehicle by the seat belt and Detective Murphy was admitted immediately into the clinic. Detective Clarke was surprised to see that Mack knew quite a few of the employees there and a thought occurred to him.

Upon this epiphany so to speak, he said, "Mack, I think I know why you don't like hospitals?"

"Oh, really, why do you think that I don't like hospitals?"

"It's because you've spent so much time in them that you feel like they give you the appearance of being weak when nothing could be further from the truth considering the fact that you are anything but weak."

"Duly noted," Mack didn't have any more of an opportunity to respond as an employee, dressed as an elf, entered in just then before saying, a mumbled "wrong room" and leaving from the door that they had just entered in from.

"It's just a couple of weeks until Christmas Day," Tyler said with a sudden realization as the thought struck him.

"Yes it is and Ms. Murphy, if you stay off that leg for a bit, it should heal up nicely, but you shouldn't do too much so that the stitches won't come out," the doctor informed Mack.

"Thanks again, Dr. Monroe."

"You're welcome and have a Merry Christmas."

"You too doctor and don't forget to order some books from me sometime."

"I won't forget because my wife will really enjoy that." Dr. Monroe left the room and Mack left the building after paying for the bill. They went to the Fairbanks Police Department where they were going to report into the chief.

Once they were there, both of the detectives went into the chief's office after knocking on the door.

Without waiting for a greeting, a smiling Detective Mackenzie said, "Hey, Chief, may I take some time off for a bit?"

"Mack, let me ask you this: are you expecting a couple of letters?"

"No. Why do you ask?"

"Here's one from the US Copyright and Patents office and this other one looks like it is from the Department of Defense. They came through the fax machine. I suppose they figured it was faster than snail mail."

"Thanks, Chief." Mack opened the letters and said, "Chief, I really need that time off because the President of the United States of America wishes to see me in Washington D.C."

"Do you know what it's about?"

"I haven't the slightest idea right now."

"Okay Detective Murphy, you can take as much time as you need to see what the president wants to see you about. I expect that Detective Clarke had better go along with you just to make sure that nothing happens to you."

"Okay, Chief, is there anything else?"

"Just get out of here Mackenzie because I think that I am catching what Mr. Tyler Clarke here calls "Mack's Madness". Right now, the crazy doesn't seem all as crazy as I think it is, which in itself is crazy."

"Then I will talk with you later, Chief." The partners exited from the room to get some things before heading to other places.

As they came out of the Fairbanks Police Department and walked nearby a Fairbanks' fabulous Christmas tree, Detective Clarke asked, "Hey Mack, how do you do what you do? Even after this long, it seems such a mystery to me."

"Come, let's take a walk." Mack led Tyler Clarke into a little coffee shop and two coffee cups were handed to her the moment they entered in. After Mack paid for the drinks, they went back to the police station. In the lobby, there was a Christmas tree with Secret Santa packages beneath it with brightly colored wrapping. Picking up one with the chief's name on it, Mack said, "See this present? Detective work is very much like determining what is in this present beneath the wrapping paper. Regardless, a person can still determine that this is a tie for the chief. It is the same with people at times because you must see past the way things seem to appear in order to discern the truth beneath the lies. It is basically seeing what is hidden and what would otherwise be unseen and that is the idea of solving puzzles and mysteries; so that you can discern the truth of the matter."

"Mack, it's just a present and not the great mysteries of the world." Detective Tyler Clarke said.

"You have to start off small in order to get a giant snowball and it's that same way with detective cases. Come with me," Detective Murphy said before she led him to one of the poorer areas of town and pulled out a package, or rather an envelope, from the inside of her jacket. Mack, with her leg still injured, set the package down and went out of sight, giving Tyler the thumbs-up sign to knock at the door. After knocking at the door, Tyler bolted out of sight behind a bush.

A woman came out and picked up the package, only to look around for someone else to claim it. Taking the package inside, it was from a living room window that the detectives watched the scene unfold within the house as a man and a woman opened the envelope. Once the envelope was actually opened, the joys and tears of the couple were infectious enough to affect the detectives watching the scene unfold before their very eyes. The effect of the moment was made even more obvious by the fact that the only decoration was a tree branch decorated like a Christmas tree.

Silently, Mack left the window. Detective Clarke realized it and took off in pursuit of the mysterious mind of Mackenzie Murphy and her "Murphy Madness". When he finally caught up to her, Tyler asked her, "How did you know about that family back there?"

"I had their daughter as one of my students and they've been struggling financially for the last couple of years. Don't tell them this, but I've been secretly helping them out for a while. The world would be a much better place if more people could help out their community and see who needs to be helped and do it. Unfortunately, people just get wrapped up in their own lives so they forget about everything and everyone else. It is a cruel, cruel world when people stop caring for others because it is caring about others that make us human."

"Mackenzie, how can you do what you do? It seems as though you hardly miss anything."

"Oh, but I do miss things because I miss relationships with friends at times since they are too busy for me living their own lives. Sometimes, when I'm alone at home, it's all I can do to keep from crying. My only simple comforts are my dogs and my journal out on the mountain trails. If I hadn't become a detective or a teacher, I should think that I would have loved to be a forest ranger." Pausing she said, "I don't know why I'm telling you this."

"That's all right. I would like to have been a forest ranger as well, but things just happened the way that they happened. I had plans, but now I just have lost dreams with only a firm plan in place for the rest of my life. That plan, Detective Mackenzie Lynn Murphy, includes you in it because without you, I'd be just another officer with a gun and a badge. You have brought meaning and purpose to my life despite anything else you say."

"Then Detective Tyler Luke Clarke, I have an answer for you."

"Did you talk with the chief about it?"

"No. Sometimes, the logical, analytical side of me prevents me from having happiness so my answer to you comes from the heart."

"What's your answer then?"

"My answer is yes because I want to spend the rest of my life with the person who loves me just as much I love him."

"Really? I thought for sure that you would say 'no' and refuse my proposal."

"There are just times that you have to unexpectedly expect the unexpected. Now let's go pack our bags because I have two tickets to Washington D.C."

"Really Mack? You make me as happy as a clam then tell me to pack my bags. It's as though you constantly try to keep me guessing."

"I'm sure that you'll figure it out or learn to deal with it, Detective." She said sweetly with a smile on her face. It was then that they noticed their location was directly under some mistletoe. For the two detectives, the possibilities for success were endless as the snow fell softly to the street where the Christmas lights lit the way.

Under the starry night sky, the aurora borealis paved the way for the dreamers' ways for yesterday, today, and tomorrow. As they softly kissed each other's lips, the northern lights showed all the peoples' hopes, dreams and sorrows. Under that sky, the possibilities were endless since the sky has no limits or bounds.

Setting forth, the detectives went to pack for the place of politics and the monotonous music of the municipal that was in the capital of the United States of America. Just before Mack left the city of Fairbanks, she filed away the case file that closed the case of the merciful murderers and their murders of mercy.

CASE 21 ACTIVITIES:

CRITICAL THINKING:

This case involves Christmas and the art of giving, although the murderers have a different idea of mercy and giving. What are some ways that you can give to others? What are some things that you do around the holidays to make them special? What was the best Christmas that you've ever had? What made it so special? Write a paper using the questions, prompted and reminiscing, about Christmas.

BONUS ACTIVITY:

Make up a gift as a special surprise to someone with no expectation of something in return. This person could be someone who you don't usually give things to or who you notice that doesn't seem to get much. It makes the gift-giving more thought provoking and more fulfilling than when you give it to someone that you give stuff to all the time.

REVIEW QUESTIONS:

1) What were the three or four case ideas that were presented to Mack? Which one did she end up choosing and why?

2) What events gave Detective Murphy the advantage over the people holding her captive after she was captured?

Why do you think they made mistakes like that? What would you have done in Detective Murphy's situation?

3) What was the epiphany that Detective Clarke had regarding Mack? (Hint: it had something to do with medicine/treatment)

4) How did Detective Murphy help out some people in her town? What would you have done in that situation?

5) What was the foreshadowing that takes place in this case? What can you guess the next case might involve?

VOCABULARY:

Define and use in a sentence based on the definition for the word.

Anonymousness-

_____

Reminiscing-

_____

VOCABULARY REVIEW:

Unscramble the word and write down the word's definition.

nyhppaei- sudden realization-_____

CASE 22:
ASSASSIN'S ATTEMPT

Trouble seemed to be Detective Mackenzie Lynn Murphy's middle name. She and Detective Clarke had been picked up at the airport by the Secret Service and someone that was familiar to both of them. The familiar face they saw was none other than that of Agent Alexandria Dawson. Agent Dawson greeted Detective Murphy by saying, "Detective Mackenzie Murphy, how have you been doing? It's been a while since I saw you last."

"Yes it has and I'm sure that you remember my partner. Upon his promotion, he is Detective Tyler Clarke now."

"Congratulations, do you have any idea why the president sent you here?"

"I haven't the slightest idea, but I wouldn't put it past Detective Murphy to know," Detective Clarke replied.

"I have a hunch, but nothing substantial as of yet."

"What's your hunch?"

"Just this," Mack said handing Agent Dawson a newspaper as she pointed out an article. The article was titled: International Investigators with a question mark as it went on to mention the idea of having an International Detective Agency setup. It would be set up in order that cases in different countries could be resolved by the specialists where an international incident was concerned. As Agent Alexandria Dawson looked at the article, a look of what Mack discerned as surprise came over her face, leaving Mackenzie to say, "Agent Dawson, just don't ask how I know what I know because I don't want to train another person to simply understand and surmise that I have "mystery madness". It's just hard for me to not analyze and discern the details of any case or crime."

"Point taken because you must be your father's daughter since details of death is Detective Matthew Murphy's specialty. Now then, the president will see you right away and then you have an invitation to have dinner at the Whitehouse with the president and the first lady."

"Do you know if the dinner will be formal or casual?"

"You'll have to ask the president that yourself. We'll be at the White House in five minutes. I can't brief you on anything that the president will say. However, I can tell you this, you'll be meeting with him outdoors."

"How's the security?"

"Top-notch, so don't worry about it, Detective Murphy, because we'll be watching out for you."

"Sorry, but is that supposed to reassure me?"

"Mack, it'll be fine. Thank you for your apparent lack of faith in other's abilities," Agent Dawson stated.

"Detectives, welcome to the White House." The driver said upon their arrival at their destination.

"Remember the last time that we were here, Mack?"

"Yes, I remember much more clearly than I would like," Detective Murphy replied, looking out the window and immediately going silent, because there was the president surrounded by a security detail of bodyguards.

He politely greeted the detectives and took the two partners for a walk before saying, "Now then Detective Mackenzie Murphy, how have you been doing?

"Decent, but what's the reason that you wanted to see us?"

"I can't fool you just like I can't fool your father, Detective Matthew Murphy."

"Well, you know what they say: I'm my father's daughter."

"That's the truth, but I'm stalling. The reason that I called you here was that I want you to be the American representation in an international detective agency known as the International Investigators Agency in which there will be representatives from all around the world. With your fame and international reputation, I believe that your abilities of deduction are exactly what this agency needs. Detective Clarke, as Detective Murphy's partner, we believed that you would be going wherever your partner would be going. It all depends on what Mackenzie wants, so do you mind if I speak alone with Detective Murphy for a few minutes?"

"Be my guest," Detective Tyler Clarke said before he left them there and Mack was left walking with the President of the United States of America.

As they walked along, the president spoke, saying, "Now Detective Murphy, what are you thinking about this job opportunity?"

"Well, I have several questions and my first question is will I have jurisdiction over all the cases that are international incidents?"

"Yes. In fact, there is an entire international detective team being formed to have jurisdiction over international incidents. You were actually recommended by another detective."

"Was that detective Detective Matthew Murphy, or some other detective that I know or possibly one that I do not know?"

"It was Detective Matthew Murphy who recommended you instead of himself as he informed me that he was getting too old to bother with something like this opportunity anymore."

"That explains quite a bit about this entire situation. Mr. President, I honestly don't see how I can trade my current detective work for international detective work because I belong in Alaska with the snow and dog sledding."

"Don't limit yourself. The possibilities for you and everyone else are infinite and you can't place limits on infinite."

"Tell me this then, Mr. President: what would you do?" Mack asked, redirecting the question to him to buy time for her response.

"I'd say yes, but at the same time, I would say no for different reasons. The important question is what will you do?" Mack slowed down, revealing the president for a second before she saw a glint of something metallic flash and rushed forward just in time to take a bullet for the president from the would-have-been assassin.

Security was instantly swarming the scene and neutralized the shooter as the president stood there stunned with a group of bodyguards around him. Mack was rushed towards a medical team as several federal and special agents arrived on the scene. All that Detective Murphy managed to mumble more to herself than anyone else was: "Some top-notch security."

Detective Clarke didn't manage to catch Mack's mumbling. He had practically sprinted to his partner's side and, as she was taken towards the hospital, he was right by her side every second that he was able to be.

A while later, Mack woke up in a bed with sheets all around her and instruments beeping. A monitor was beeping in a rhythmic time, keeping to the beating of her heart. It was apparent where she was and as she reflected back to find out the reason why she was in there, she remembered what had happened to place her in this current predicament. Detective Mackenzie Murphy had actually taken a bullet for the president without being a bodyguard or the average person expected to risk their life and limb for the commander and chief of the entire country.

Unfortunately, the bullet that she had taken had missed the vest and had lodged itself in her shoulder, affecting the shoulder's socket. The bullet had been extracted, but the possibility of surgery loomed in the detective's near future if all went according to the doctor's plan. Mackenzie knew of this without talking with a nurse or a doctor within the hospital. There were a couple of X-rays that indicated her shoulder's condition. Just then, interrupting her musings, a nurse entered into the room and said, "It's nice to see that you're awake. You've become rather famous around here in the hospital so I must ask if what I heard was true."

"If what's true? What did you hear?" Mack said, playing ignorance.

"Did you really solve all those cases and save the president's life from an assassination attempt?"

"Did you really get engaged recently?"

"Yes, but how did you know about that?"

"You just barely have the indication of a ring being on your engagement finger, which means that it must be a recent occurrence." Mack said, not acknowledging her recent engagement.

"Yes, it was. That means that you are as good as they say you are."

Just then, a doctor came in and said, "Nurse, we need to prep the detective for surgery on that shoulder, but before we do that, there's someone here to see you, Ms. Murphy." The doctor briefly stuck his head out of the room and nodded.

It wasn't long before Detective Tyler Clarke entered into the room and said, "Hey Mack, it always seems like I am the one worrying about you whenever you get shot. Good luck in your surgery and I'd have you know that the president wants to honor you for saving his life once you get better."

"I'd prefer to not be honored as my being honored, if that makes any sense. There are plenty of people out there who could use that type of recognition other than me because there are plenty of heroes out there. I just have an excellent sense of timing and I don't save lives for recognition or to be honored. I save lives for the saving, because they need to be saved in one form or another."

"I don't think that there is anything you can do to dissuade the president on this matter," he stated.

"There is one thing. . ." Just then, the nurse interrupted to have Detective Clarke leave the room so that Detective Murphy could go into surgery. They gave her an anesthetic and the last thing that she remembered seeing was two double doors that they were going through to go towards the surgery room.

When she finally woke up from the anesthetic, Mackenzie wasn't in the hospital and there was a metal table nearby with a man in a black suit behind it. Placing a light brown envelop on the table, there was black lettering on it addressed to Detective Mackenzie Murphy. Speaking with all-due formality, the man in the black suit went on to say, "Detective Murphy, we require your services to solve a matter of uncertainty with a case. You won't have your shoulder surgery until you solve it."

"Really? Well, unfortunately for you, I don't take candy or cases from strangers."

"We've met briefly once before, but it was hardly a noteworthy encounter. I was called Hawk Black and I was the pilot during that situation quite a while ago where the helicopter went down. The reason that you're here is to solve what I believe to be the murder of a fellow pilot of mine and here's the case file for you."

"All right, I'll check it out." Detective Murphy said as she picked up the envelope and opened it to reveal the case in question. The contents, which were papers and photos within the envelope, revealed that a pilot had died as a result of that pilot's lack of judgment rather than a mechanical malfunction as it had been previously believed.

The detail of the case that caught Mackenzie's eye was the not-quite-so-obvious obviousness about the inaccuracies of the photographs. The maker of the mechanical equipment in question was a large corporation making millions by making the aviation engines for aircrafts. Had any issue been presented, such as a mechanical failure case such as this was, they stood to lose a great deal of money. That fact alone proved that this case had been covered up in order to keep the greedy corporation content.

After analyzing and drawing conclusions, Mack finally laid down two photographs, side-by-side, in front of "Hawk Black" as his code name had been. It was then that she said, "These photographs don't add up and do you know why? It is because these aren't the same engine parts that were in the aircraft. Granted, they appear quite similar, however, upon closer inspection, they're not quite the same."

"You're right, but why didn't anyone else notice this about these photographs?"

"It's probably because they didn't have me to look them over. However, there are several possibilities. First, there could have been a pay-off or the inquiry could have been corrupted before it even started. No matter how you look at it, that corporation got away with murder. What we'll have to do is call for a retrial in order to prove that the error really was mechanical."

"Now how are we supposed to do that?"

"We have to acquire both of these engines and test them out to see if it'll do the same thing that your pilot friend experienced."

"I don't know about you, but I just don't have an extra twenty-five thousand lying around anywhere."

"Thankfully for you, I do have such funds readily available to me. Could I get a laptop or a computer in here?" Mackenzie asked.

"I'll bring one right in," Hawk Black said before he left the room for a moment, leaving Detective Murphy alone within the confines of four white walls that seemed to be closing in on her. This certainly emphasized the point of why she disliked hospitals and her thoughts returned back to her partner, Detective Clarke for a moment.

In the meantime, Detective Clarke was being informed by a nurse about the current situation after the hospital confirmed it. The nurse nervously played with a pen as she said, "I regret to inform you that Detective Mackenzie Murphy is missing."

"How can you lose a detective in a hospital?"

"We're not sure because it could only have happened between the room that she was in and the operating room. Beyond that, we have no idea about the particulars of what happened to her. We'll let you know whether or not there's any other information on the matter," the nurse replied before leaving the room without waiting for any further response from Detective Clarke.

Agent Alexandria Dawson tried to console Detective Tyler Clarke by saying, "We'll find her. It's not like she hasn't escaped from a hospital before, so we'll find her."

"What I'm worried about is the fact that she was put under with an anesthetic before going to the operating room. Mackenzie has taught me enough to know that such a thing implies foul play and not the act of a brilliant madness by Mack, "He explained.

"What do you suggest?" Agent Dawson asked.

"That we request to review the surveillance and get to the bottom of this detective disappearance," Detective Clarke demanded.

"What do you think happened to Detective Murphy?" Agent Dawson asked.

"I try not to speculate about any of Mack's madness anymore. No matter what, Mackenzie Murphy and her father, Matthew Murphy, continually surprise me," Detective Clarke explained.

"That's the truth about the matter, now let's go figure out what happened to Mackenzie." They approached security to see about the surveillance tapes and find out the truth behind the detective's disappearance. They put the surveillance tapes into a machine that projected them over a security monitor so that the detective and agent could view them with relative ease.

Meanwhile, someone else was looking at a computer monitor with considerable focus and determination in order to solve a case for the people holding her hostage. Purchasing two different engines, Detective Murphy asked for the address that they would be sent before putting the engines on next-day shipping. After that was taken care of, she started compiling the necessary paperwork to take in front of a judge. When she had that taken care of, Mack wrote down her phone number for Hawk Black just in case there was anything else as she said, "I know that you'll have to return me for my surgery. This is my number so you can call me to finish this case or if you need any more of my help in the future. All I ask is that you just let me know that you need my help next time instead of stealing me away for my services."

"Definitely sounds like a plan and much easier than this stunt was too. Sorry, Detective, but we have to put you back under with an anesthetic before we can take you back."

"That's all right, do what you have to do because I'm ready." Mack had just barely finished saying that before she felt the sensation of a needle prick. The last thing she saw was that she was heading out an open door into the unknown.

The next thing she knew, she was on a gurney in the morgue under a white sheet. Mack threw off the sheet and sat up, making the mortician in the room drop his sandwich to the morgue's floor tiles. When Detective Murphy spoke, saying, "Could you take me to Detective Clarke and the person with him please?"

"Noooooooo!" The mortician yelled as he fled from the room, thinking that he had seen a ghost or a hallucination. After the mortician left in such a hurry, Detective Mackenzie Murphy got off of the gurney and went up a nearby staircase to the third level. While the mortician called into security, frantically trying to explain that a corpse was alive, Mack was safely climbing the stairs to the hospital above.

The security officer responded by saying, "I think that you need to take a break. You must be starting to see things down there in the morgue. That is the most ridiculous thing I've heard all day: a corpse getting up and walking away."

"Why don't you take a break or do your job. I was taking a break when this incident happened. In fact, my sandwich is still on the floor. Why don't you take a break you lazy security officers?" The mortician was angry enough that he hung up the phone.

The security probably would have been tempted to take a break, however, that was when the security officer at the monitor noticed something and played back the footage at the morgue. After seeing the footage, the officer said, "Uh, sir, you have to see this because it is unbelievable."

"What now?" The chief supervising security officer responded before the footage was played back before his very eyes.

That was when security called the morgue back and apologized to the mortician there saying, "Sorry, we have just reviewed the footage and you did actually see a body get up and walk away from the morgue. We apologize for any doubt that we might have first expressed and we are looking into the situation."

"Thank you for believing me. What you can do to help me is find the person or whatever you can call this." The mortician was thinking of zombies at this point only because of watching too much television and movies where the dead walk.

"We'll try and find whoever or whatever that you can call a corpse becoming alive." Security hung up the phone to find the person behind the morgue mystery. Meanwhile,

Detective Murphy went to a receptionist's desk and located her nurse, who was quite surprised to see Ms. Mackenzie Murphy unharmed inside the hospital. The first thing the nurse did was to prepare her for the shoulder operation, personally escorting her to the operating room before informing Detective Clarke and Agent Dawson that Detective Murphy had been found, leaving them full of questions; questions that wouldn't be answered until Mack came back out of the operation room after her surgery.

This was confirmed when she finally came out of the operation room where she had been for an hour, much longer than anyone had anticipated. Officer Tyler Clarke and Agent Dawson were finally able to see Mack when she was lying in a hospital bed after the operation with the effects of the operation and medicine still evident. For Mackenzie, it was what she disliked with absolute certainty and that was the worst torture that anyone could ever inflict upon her.

Officer Clarke just had to grin, seeing Mackenzie's misery and the fact that only Mack Murphy could become a missing person in a hospital while under an anesthetic. In all of his experience, there was only one person who could manage an incident like this under such circumstances and that person was now in the hospital bed in front of Tyler Clarke. Still, there was a burning question that he just had to ask of her. "Mack, what happened to you?"

"I just solved a case is all and it was no big deal. In the future, they'll ask before they take me without permission. However, I must admit that I'm surprised that you didn't send in the FBI or the CIA to locate me."

"We had initially thought that it was just some cruel idea of a hospital hoax until we saw the footage with our own eyes. As usual, you were just too fast for us to even start trying to find you before we would be able to call in the other agencies that you just mentioned. We didn't have time to figure out the: who, what, why, and how questions about the case. Can we know the details of what happened to you now?"

"Sorry, but Ms. Murphy needs to rest. She'll probably be released tomorrow, if all goes well. You can talk with her then," the nurse said. In response, Detective Clarke left the room with Agent Dawson, leaving Detective Murphy to sleep and recover before she was able to be released from the hospital.

When she was released in the morning, Detective Tyler Clarke and Agent Alexandria Dawson escorted her to an awaiting vehicle in the parking lot. Once they were inside the car, Agent Dawson said, "The president wants to have breakfast with us this morning so we are headed to the White House right now."

"Thanks, I already figured that we were, but it's always nice to be told by someone else to confirm a hypothesis."

Once they were at the White House and had breakfast, the president took Mackenzie Murphy aside to speak with her about his previous proposition by saying, "Detective Murphy, have you given any thought about joining the International Investigatory Agency?"

"I have, Mr. President."

"What decision have you made?"

"I've come to the conclusion and decided to decline the offer. However, I can be available as an advisor if the International Investigatory Agency needs any assistance on any of their cases."

"There's something that you should know before you set your decision in stone and that is the fact that Detective Clarke has already accepted a position in the International Investigatory Agency. Do you want to change your mind now or are you set on your current decision about the matter?"

"I've had enough problems getting injured on Alaskan cases so I can't honestly accept a position where I'd feel out of my element. That means that I will prefer to stay with my current decision and stay available as an advisor instead. I just can't accept it with a clear conscience, knowing that I would more than likely be the face of the International Investigatory Agency rather than participate as an active detective in the cases."

"That's why your father wouldn't join, along with the fact that he said that such things were for the younger generation to deal with. Also, there is one other thing that I would like to mention at this time and that is the fact that I never had the opportunity to properly thank you for taking a bullet for me. It's not often that someone as respectable as you takes a bullet for a president and for that, I'm eternally grateful. Thank you."

"Mr. President, I'm sure that anyone would do the same thing as I did if given the opportunity and I'm sure that someone would do the same thing for me."

"Still, Detective Murphy, you're a hero in my book." the president said.

"That's what they tell me: that I'm a hero, but honestly, there are a lot of heroes out there and I would much rather be known as I actually am; a person just trying to do what's right. Now will we be able to get back to Alaska or do you want me to join another one of your organizations?"

"No, you'll be free to go back to Alaska, if you wish. Thank you, Detective Murphy; you really helped us in this matter, even if you might not think so."

"You're welcome Mr. President, but I didn't do much except refuse your offer, save your life, and one other exciting adrenaline-pumping experience from this entire trip."

Detective Murphy rejoined Detective Clarke and Agent Dawson as they headed back to the Washington D.C. airport, prompting Agent Dawson to ask, "Did you have a good time?"

"As best as possible under the circumstances," Mack replied.

It wasn't until they were on the airplane headed home without Agent Dawson that detectives Clarke and Murphy were able to have a frank discussion amongst partners of their visit, confiding in each other. The discussion started off with Detective Clarke saying, "Hey, Mack, did the president inform you that I accepted a position at the International Investigatory Agency?"

"Yes, as a matter of fact, he did mention something like that. What do you think about it?"

"I think that we'd be unstoppable at the international investigations."

"There's just one problem. I won't be on it. However, I will be an advisor for the international investigations if and when they need my advice."

"Why's that? I thought for sure that you would join, which is why I joined."

"They would only have me as a figurehead for the agency because of my fame and I just couldn't live with that. I would be solving cases like I am, but it would all be under the microscope. I couldn't stand it and because of the fact that I'd miss Alaska too much to put up with such publicity for too long.

"Then this probably means that we won't get married now because I never do well in long-distance relationships."

"So it would seem and I'm sorry that it couldn't work out. It's probably my fault, but I just couldn't accept the position knowing that I could be miserable."

"A miserable Mackenzie Murphy is someone that I don't want to meet. It's bad enough that I have to deal with a "mad" Murphy." Detective Clarke said grinning.

Mack replied by saying, "Neither would I and I don't want to meet a miserable Detective Clarke either or a mad Clarke."

"Yes, I think that it would make me considerably less miserable if you kept the ring that I gave you. You might need it someday, Detective Murphy, but this also means that we'll both get a new partner." Detective Clarke said in a feeble attempt to try and make the situation less awkward than it already was.

With nothing else to say that could be said, Mackenzie took a pen and paper to say what could not be said aloud in a way that was not black and white, but was in a way that all could determine with a discerning eye the feelings coursing through her. There was only one problem with what was said, and that was the fact that there was a sense of secrecy because not many would know what the pen name of Detective Mackenzie Murphy would be. Whether she would ever be a famous writer or not someday was still uncertain, but what was certain was the fact that the case was solved and that tomorrow would be just another day in history. It was the people throughout the public who defined history; however, it was still a mystery to be solved by Detective Mackenzie Lynn Murphy. There are many mysteries in life, but only one mysterious Mack Murphy.

CASE 22 ACTIVITIES:

CRITICAL THINKING:

As a direct result of Detective Murphy saving the president's life from an assassination attempt, she is considered a hero. Who are some average everyday heroes? What makes them heroes? Most people think of superman or wonder woman as heroes. How does the appearance of average heroes compare to the idea presented by those superheroes? Write a paper about your own personal hero in your life, exemplifying the qualities that make that person a hero to you.

REVIEW QUESTIONS:

1) What is the International Detective Agency that Mack infers is the reason behind their visit to the White House? What is the title that the president gives to that agency idea?

2) Would you have taken a bullet for the president if you were in Detective Murphy's situation? Why or Why not?

3) Why was Detective Murphy taken out of the hospital and what was the case that she was presented with in the hopes of solving it?

4) What was Detective Murphy's answer towards the president's request regarding the detective agency? How did this compare to Detective Clarke's answer? What was

the significance of their decisions and what might happen to the detective duo as a result?

VOCABULARY:

Define and use in a sentence based on the definition for the word.

Jurisdiction-_____

Dissuade-

_____

Anesthetic-

_____

Exemplifying-

_____

VOCABULARY REVIEW:

Unscramble the word and write down the word's definition.

Eiurssm – determine

_____

Rroeucp- reveal; make appear

_____

CASE 23:
CAMPING CHAOS

Detective Mack Murphy, as she was known, put together her gear for a much-needed camping trip with her famous father, Detective Matthew Murphy. She had turned down the president's offer of a position at the International Investigatory Agency, or IIA as its acronym was. Instead she chose to be available as an advisor if it was needed.

Due to a difference in communication and understanding amongst the partners, Detective Clarke ended up joining the IIA which successfully divided the partners up into two different organizations. It seemed that those differences at this time, were irreparable and it was partly because of these problems that Detective Matthew Murphy had suggested this camping trip. Because of this suggestion, Mack had packed some case files and some other appropriate reading material for the prospective adventure, such as a couple of books. These, she felt, could entertain her because of what camping with her father entailed.

Putting her pack and gear in the truck, she then waited, pen and notebook in hand, for her dad to come out of the house and be ready to face up to the challenges ahead of them, whatever those challenges might be. When Detective Matthew Murphy finally did appear, he set a couple of packs down, looking at the space in the truck before saying, "Mackenzie, why'd you only bring one pack for this trip? You don't have to travel light for this trip."

"I have everything I need. Even if you pack light, you just have to pack prepared for any and all situations. I'm fairly certain that I do have everything I need and I've just gotten rather use to packing light, but prepared."

"Have it your way. It's not like we're solving a murder or anything like that."

"That's right. Wait...we aren't; are we? Solving a murder while camping?"

"No, we're not solving a murder so you just need to relax right now. Just relax Kenzie for once in your life."

"I thought that you always called me Mack. What happened to that because I'm more comfortable with that nickname?"

"Sorry, but your mother insisted that I refer to you like the lady you are. Speaking of which, what happened between you and your partner, Detective Clarke?"

"I'd rather not say so let's just go camping."

"That sounds great to me. What do you have for the radio?"

"I have some country music that ya'll like or at least I figured that you would like some of it."

"Then let's go because daylight's wasting." Detective Matthew Murphy said, following the western themed conversation.

Without any hesitation, Mack climbed into the SUV, with a grin saying, "We're probably the only ones in Idaho going camping during the first week in February just to relax and unwind."

"Probably, but that just means that we'll have the trails to ourselves."

"Hopefully, because I think that it'll just be relaxing to take a break from murders and mysteries for a while."

"Yes it will, especially considering the fact that it's been a while since we've done something like this. Let's just have fun Mackenzie." With nothing else to be said, their attention was turned towards the road passing beneath the tires, successfully diverting their attention from the awkwardness of the conversation to their own inward problems, not exhibited by outward expressions. With their focus on the road ahead of them, they drove towards their destination: Lost Valley Reservoir, nearby the little town of Council, Idaho. Detective Matthew Murphy had a cabin not far from the reservoir, but there was only one problem with the reservoir. How could a reservoir have any problems with it? The name wasn't the only issue or problem that Mack Murphy had to contend with because there were other words that came to symbolize the detective's kryptonite, in a manner of speaking.

While Detectives Matthew and Mackenzie Murphy were making their way to Council, Detective Clarke was making his way to the border of the United States and Canada where a corpse had been disassembled across the border with evidence of human remains on both sides. The state of the United States in question just happened to be Idaho, leaving Detective Clarke unwittingly thinking of his previous partner before turning back towards the dilemma at hand. It was a dilemma because of the fact that there was no suspect in the vicinity so that the services of a detective, in this case Detective Clarke and the IIA (International Investigatory Agency) were required.

In and amongst the pine trees, they worked compiling evidence that would hopefully lead to the arrest of a murderer. Detective Clarke was so set in his pursuit to compile evidence that he almost didn't notice or realize that there was a business card for the Pine Lodge in Council, Idaho where Detective Matthew Murphy lived. It was as he turned back to the task at hand that he had an epiphany or, rather, a sudden realization of what the business card meant due to the previous conversation with a famous detective.

The day before this case, Detective Matthew Murphy had informed Detective Tyler Clarke of his intention to go to Council for the weekend. It was then that Tyler could only hope fervently that he would be able to reach him once they got service and that they would stay away from the Pine Lodge nearby the road leading up to Lost Valley Reservoir.

For the meantime, Detective Clarke logged the business card as evidence as they took pictures and gathered together all the pieces of the corpse. All the little details and items that the investigation team gathered were considered evidence and any little miniscule detail could make or break the case. However, by the time that Detective Clarke found the business card, Detectives Matthew and Mackenzie Murphy were already making camp at Lost Valley Reservoir.

As mentioned before, it was somewhat of a coincidence that Pine Lodge was just down the road from Lost Valley Reservoir. As they made their camp, it provided a false sense of security because an unknown danger was in the form of a person setting up camp just across the body of water.

Despite all of this false sense of security, Detective Mackenzie Murphy found that she was relaxing while reading some writing material that was very motivational and relaxing. After only a few minutes of this, father and daughter brought into action a couple of snowmobiles that they brought with them, tearing up the snow as they sped down the trail. At least they were until the two detectives heard the resounding blast of a gunshot and saw a deer stagger in front of them.

Pretty soon, a person came up, only to be confronted by Detective Mackenzie Murphy, who said, "This is not hunting season so that act of killing is considered poaching around these parts." Cuffs were placed on the person's hands until they were able to report the poacher to the Fish and Game as the guilty person he was. Little did they know that they had just captured the notorious Hunting Hunger of the Hills and had more problems waiting for them.

They called into the Fish and Game, receiving a response in which a representative from the establishment came with an officer from the Adams County Sherriff's Office about forty-five minutes after the initial communication had been made. One of representatives said, "Hi, I believe that you mentioned the fact that you found a poacher?"

"Yes. We heard a gunshot before a deer staggered in front of us, followed by this man. I must say that the deer looks like a nice buck with a large rack, a seven point buck if I'm not mistaken."

"Who are you to be such a good citizen?"

"I'm Detective Mackenzie Murphy and this is my father, Detective Matthew Murphy."

"What are you doing up here in the first place?"

"We're camping and my daughter is on vacation at the moment. We could give you our statements if need be about this matter," Detective Matthew Murphy offered.

"That won't be necessary. I just can't believe that I'm actually meeting the world-famous Detective Matthew Murphy in person. I must say that it's an honor."

"Before you take him, you might look at that photo in his back pocket." The officer looked at what Detective Mack Murphy had pointed out and, sure enough, there was a photo in the man's back pants pocket. The photo looked similar to one shown on the news, making the officer say, "I believe that you just captured the Hunting Hunger of the Hills, Detectives. Congratulations on your latest achievement of deduction."

"Thanks, but we didn't really do that much except to be at the right place at the right time."

"Sometimes, that's all that it takes. Thanks again, Detectives."

"You're welcome, but do us a favor and don't mention us when it is publicized, otherwise, we might have problems."

"Sure thing, now come along, George Dailey. You have to account for your criminal actions and accept responsibility for the consequences. Under no circumstances is poaching tolerated or even accepted." The officer and poacher left without any further conversation.

Once they were far enough away, the Fish and Game representative said, "This is definitely a fresh kill considering the fact that it is still warm. Could you help me get it back to my vehicle? I would greatly appreciate it."

"No problem." They helped bring the deer back to the Fish and Game vehicle before they headed back to their campsite.

They had lunch before they headed towards an access road that would lead them to a road outside of Council and nearby Starkey's Hot Springs. That road led off towards the little town of Fruitvale, Idaho. All of this was on their snowmobiles; at least, it was until Detective Matthew Murphy's snow machine slipped off a slick snow bank that caused the machine to get stuck in the snow, pitching him off. He slid until he was stopped with his leg somewhat less intact than it previously had been before the incident and that was when the fun really started.

Mack took her dad back to camp by towing her father's snowmobile along with him immobilized on the seat. They arrived at the camp and she called for medical services before her father said, "Hey Mack, don't let this ruin your weekend. Stay here and try to relax as you write in your notebook."

"All right, Dad. I won't let it ruin my weekend, but I'm sorry that you ended up getting hurt on this camping trip because that was not my intention."

"It wasn't my intent either, but at least we caught the Hunting Hunger of the Hills and had some fun on the snowmobiles. I'm proud of you, Mackenzie."

"Thanks. I thought that, whatever I did, it couldn't compare to what my brother did. I felt you just couldn't be proud of me no matter what."

"Mackenzie, I was proud of you, but you seemed so self-confident that I didn't need to say that I was proud of you. I thought that there was nothing for me to say because you already understood. It wasn't that I didn't love you or wasn't proud of you, because I was and always will be. It was on behalf of your brother that I did that, because I love you and I'm proud of you."

"Thanks, Dad that means a lot, especially coming from you. I just hope that your leg will heal up good."

"It will. They can't keep either of us down for long since it's only a broken leg." Matthew smiled at his daughter before the ambulance arrived seconds later and Detective Murphy was taken away with the flashing lights shining in their whirling motion as he was driven towards the most convenient medical facility to handle a broken leg, which ended up being McCall, Idaho.

As they left, Mack sat back down, alternating between reading a book that she had brought with her and writing with a pen in her notebook. However, that was interrupted when she heard the snow crunching nearby.

A man appeared out of seemingly nowhere with a hand in one of his pockets and Mack was instantly on her guard as he introduced himself. The man's name sounded kind of familiar and Detective Mack Murphy had a feeling that it was because the man was a criminal rather than a cop. Her suspicions were confirmed when she saw a glint of steel, that just so happened to be a gun, in the waistband of his snow pants. Mack politely introduced herself without her detective title before she tried to have him leave by looking disinterested in his company. However, that just escalated the problem. The man ended up pulling out his gun and with a malicious smile, he said, "Mackenzie Murphy, you are coming with me. In fact, like all the others, you don't have a choice in the matter."

"Great, just let me take this pen and journal with me, in my back pocket." Mack said as she placed the articles into her back pocket and followed where the man led her.

Meanwhile, Detective Clarke called the famous Detective Matthew Murphy on his cell phone. Matt Murphy answered saying, "Hello, this is Detective Matthew Murphy speaking."

"Hey Matthew, where's Mack?"

"She's still camping, but I'm not at the moment because I have a broken leg. Why? What's up?"

"There's a suspect nearby the Pine Lodge not far from Council so I was just making sure that she was doing all right, but if she's camping then she's fine."

"Not necessarily, since Mackenzie is camping at Lost Valley Reservoir, which isn't far from the Pine Lodge."

"Why didn't you say so? The suspect checked out of the Pine Lodge and was reported heading up that direction. Mack could be in trouble as we speak and there is not a really good way of reaching her."

"Knowing my daughter, she probably is in trouble. However, Mackenzie doesn't get into any trouble that she can't handle."

"Knowing your daughter, Sir, there is seemingly no amount of trouble that she can't handle. I'm in love with your daughter and yes, I'm rather stressed at the moment, but I'm in love with her."

"Now you figure it out, and Detective, she is in love with you even if she won't admit it. I'll just tell you this one thing: go rescue her Detective Clarke and do something right today."

"Yes, Sir, I will. Thank you, Mr. Murphy."

"Just call me Matthew, but you're welcome. Now go get Mackenzie before she is murdered." Detective Clarke hung up and told the driver to drive faster. As luck would have it, they managed to get stuck in the snow right by where someone was taking their dog sled team out. Detective Clarke got a grin on his face before he asked, "Could I borrow your dog sled team to rescue someone? Someone I know is in trouble and I really could use a dog sled team right now to help with the matter. I promise that I'll return everything and all the dogs in one piece."

"Sure, I just hope that you know what you're doing."

"I come from Alaska and I grew up around sled dogs and mushing so I would say that I know exactly what I'm doing regarding this aspect. Thanks." The musher acknowledged him with a nod as Detective Clarke took the team up the trail to rescue his former partner, Detective Mackenzie Lynn Murphy.

It was as he was going down the trail that he heard a gunshot ringing out in the winter's cold. It prompted him to pull out his own pistol, turning the team towards the direction of the gunshot. When he came to the scene of the shot, Mack was there holding her head with crimson staining the snow. A man loomed over her, holding a gun saying, "Now Mackenzie Murphy, you shall die before me."

"Freeze! Drop the gun! I said drop the gun now you, for the lack of a better word, monster." Detective Clarke said, holding a gun to him.

The man responded by saying, "You first, Detective. Ms. Murphy here can't do anything to help you." While the man's attention was directed towards Detective Clarke, Mack pulled out a Taser and the man just barely directed his attention back to her as she fired it off, getting shot in the chest before releasing the trigger.

Detective Clarke cuffed the culprit before he checked on Detective Mack Murphy once more by saying, "Mack? Are you going to be fine or do you need an ambulance?"

"I was wearing my vest, but a bullet grazed my head. Get the first aid kit out of the SUV. It should be on the floor by the passenger seat in a yellow box."

"I got it, Mack! I'll be right back." Detective Clarke left, returning with the yellow box that housed the first aid and he helped bandage the wound on her head with gentle care. As he worked on her head, he said, "Thank you for your assistance, Mack. What's the plan?"

"I already loaded up the snow machines and everything onto the trailer. The SUV is already packed. Since I'm in no state to drive the vehicle back at all, here are the keys. I'll take the dog sled team back, but I'll have to go in front of you when going down the road."

"Okay, Mack. That sounds like a plan. You can head towards the place above Council with the Pine or should I say the Pine Lodge." Mack nodded her head as she stood on the runners and they went back towards Pine Lodge where they ended up meeting with the musher and the other people helping with the International Investigatory Agency's investigation.

The musher greeted her team with enthusiasm before inquiring, "Are you Detective Mackenzie Murphy?"

"Yes, I am, but what makes you ask that?"

"I'm a huge fan. In fact, I want to go to Alaska someday in order to race in the Iditarod."

"What's your name?"

"Katy Watson."

"What would you say about helping me during the Iditarod? You would be helping my current handler and I'd pay for your round trip flight to and from Alaska."

"What do you say, Dad? Can I please do that?"

"I don't see why not, just so long as you are able to do it with your school schedule."

"Well, here's my business card and I will mainly need your help before the race because that is the busiest time for me. Once out on the trail, it is where the training is put into practice for me and my team." Mack handed Katy a business card before she was escorted to another IIA vehicle waiting for them as Detective Clarke and the culprit, the notorious, "Wicked Woodsman"; William "Willie Jack-Jax, were escorted with them.

It was another chaotic case that just found them, as trouble always does, rather than the detective finding the troublesome case. As Mack relaxed, however ill-at-ease she was about the prospective appointment in her favorite place, the hospital, she fell asleep. In fact, she was so tired that, at their destination, she was still sleeping as the prisoner was taken away to the "prison" for international criminals like what Willie was.

Detective Clarke knew that he had to leave and left a note in Mack's pocket without waking her up from her slumber. Even as Detective Clarke left, "Mad" Mackenzie Murphy dreamed of mushing the Iditarod trail with a golden glow from her headlamp's light shining through a wall of white snow as they pressed onward. Pressing onward through the conditions and fatigue of mushing, they sought the solace and sleep that would be provided at the checkpoint. The dog team and musher were now making that destination their goal and aim to reach. Everything else wasn't visible like the shining light in the window of the next checkpoint because even the impossible is possible.

CASE 23 ACTIVITIES:

CRITICAL THINKING:

This case mentions the fact that they bring some supplies with them on their camping trip; what supplies do you think they took with them for this trip? What supplies would you have taken with you on the camping trip? What was the best camping trip that you've been on? What things made it great? What things could have gone differently to make it even better? Write a paper about the camping trip or what you would do on a camping trip if given the opportunity to go on one.

REVIEW QUESTIONS:

1) What was the original objective of the trip for Mackenzie? Why did that objective fail?

2) Who were the people responsible for the devious deeds mentioned in this case?

3) How did Detective Clarke get involved with the situation? Why do you think there was that connection between the case and the camping trip?

4) Why did the detectives bring snow machines with them on a camping trip? How did this make their trip more enjoyable or add to the adverse adventurer accounts?

5) What could have made that ordeal with the criminal turn out better? In what ways could it have turned out worse?

6) What would it be like to be behind a dog team? If you were the musher in that instance, would you have let the detective take your dog team? Why or why not?

VOCABULARY:

Define and use in a sentence based on the definition for the word.

Acronym-

_____

Irreparable-

_____

Miniscule-

_____

Notorious-

_____

CASE 24:
MUSHING MADNESS

Through the swirling mist of snow, a dog sled team appeared from the wall of white. A person frantically waved at the approaching dog sled team and the snow crunched as the sled slid to a halt. The musher pressed the snow hooks soundly into the silvery snow in the snow storm and the musher stepped off of the runners.

Suddenly, a knife blade gleamed in what light there was by headlamp or flashlight. Surprise wrought the person's features underneath the cold weather gear as the musher fell down on the ground. Thick, rich, crimson blood stained the untainted sparkling snow as the unknown person fled the scene of the crime on dog sled rather than snowmobile so as to not draw attention to the deed that was done as though it was a deadly duty.

It was quite accidental that the next person to appear on the horizon was the musher, Mackenzie Murphy. The musher was also a detective for the Fairbanks Police Department with her previous partner in the International Investigators' Agency. The body was covered in a layering of snow and it was by no surprise that, upon checking for a pulse, there was none to be found.

Detective Murphy took out a camera taking pictures, knowing that this was a crime scene. Mack pulled out her cell phone and called Detective Tyler Luke Clarke of the International Investigators' Agency or the IIA as it's known. The phone ringing in her ear was picked up on the other end and she said, "Hi, this is Detective Murphy and I need to speak to Detective Clarke."

"What's up? This is Detective Tyler Clarke at your service."

"Are you out of earshot of everyone else, Tyler?"

"Yes, but why?"

"It's because of what I'm about to tell you and the fact that it needs to remain completely confidential other than a select few people. I will also need you to inform the Iditarod Trail Dog Sled Race Officials of this current predicament."

"All right, Mack. You can trust me. What do you want to tell me?"

"A musher has been murdered on the Iditarod Trail."

"Are you serious?"

"When it comes to murder, I'm completely serious."

"All right; I believe you, but who was killed?"

"The musher was wearing bib number nineteen from Canada."

"That makes this an international incident and the International Investigators' Agency has the case rather than the Alaska State Police or any other Alaska Police department."

"Just keep in touch and let me know what the plan is."

"I will do that. Mack, you be safe out there and watch yourself."

"I will. I'll talk with you later."

"Okay, bye Mack." Mackenzie Murphy pulled her team up ahead of the victim and gave each of the dogs a snack and some well-deserved water. After covering the corpse, she took a walk around the area. Dog sled tracks led away from the scene of the crime, but the most useful clue was something that had dropped five feet up the trail. It was a bag and Mack took a picture of it before examining the contents. Inside the bag was a knife with blood on it and a wallet. Obviously, it was accidentally dropped in the culprit's haste to get away. These two clues would also be the criminal's undoing regarding the murder.

About a half an hour later, a snowmobiler came up wearing an International Investigators Agent uniform. The person dismounted from the snow machine and Mack instantly liked him for some reason. He pulled out his identification after he pulled out his notebook with a universal pen that would write almost anywhere. Speaking, he said, "Hi, I'm David Danner with the International Investigators Agency. I was on vacation when Detective Clarke contacted me to come down here. What exactly is the situation?"

"We have a victim, the murder weapon, and the culprit's identity, I believe. The victim is a musher with bib number nineteen from Canada and here is his identification."

"No wonder Detective Clarke said that you're one of the best if not the best." Just then, another snowmobile pulled up with Detective Clarke riding on it.

Once he dismounted after shutting off the snow machine, he said, "Hi Mack, it's nice to see you and I see that you've met David. He's been working with me lately although I must admit that I miss all the excitement I had while working with you, Detective."

Mack nodded in acknowledgement of what he said before she went back to her team, leaving David to show Detective Clarke the clues that Mackenzie had previously found. After she came back to where the two were working, Detective Clarke said, "Mack, this fellow we are looking for is also running in the Iditarod so be careful out there. We're going to secure the crime scene and wait for back-up to arrive."

"That sounds good. This culprit has about half an hour on you so you should keep that in mind, Tyler. It was nice meeting you Mr. Danner." Mack readied her team and changed her direction in order to follow the culprit's tracks in the snow as the marks of a dog sled's runners stretched out before her. It was kind of comical, because of the fact that she was racing to solve a murder right in the middle of the Iditarod Trail Dog Sled Race.

As she went along down the path with her dog sled team, the lead dog followed the scent of the other team along with the tracks. As they ran, the snow continued to fall down in all its white splendor as Detective Murphy pursued the tracks on the back of a dog sled to the unknown destination. About half an hour later, the tracks returned to the Official Iditarod Trail with the trail markers showing them the way. Once back on the trail, Mack's team practically flew and they came across another musher who was stopped off of the trail.

As a detective, Mackenzie Murphy noticed details about the musher that most people would have missed. It was by these details that Mack inferred the musher's guilt on the matter even while approaching the musher and stopping her team behind his. It was on this basis that she searched through her sled bag as though she were looking for something before she asked the other musher, "Hey, I can't seem to find my knife and I need to use it to break up some snacks for my dogs that appear to be frozen together. Could you lend me a knife? I just need to use it, and then I'll give it right back to you."

"Just so long as you give it right back and don't try any funny business."

"I will give it right back and I won't try anything with it." The other musher nodded before he realized that his pack was gone that had the murder weapon in it before he regained his composure and improvised, giving Mack a sheathed buck knife to use. Detective Murphy pretended to use it and wiped it off before returning the knife to its rightful owner.

That's when things turned ugly because the other musher got a glimpse of a badge. The musher pulled out a pistol and said, "You're a cop, aren't you?"

"I'm a detective."

"Hold it right there then."

"Why? It's not like you've done anything wrong and even if you had, I'm a musher right now so I'm not working."

"It doesn't matter, you've seen my face and I can't leave any witnesses." Two shots were fired in rapid succession, hitting Detective Murphy in the chest before the culprit fled the scene.

Another musher had been a ways off and saw the act happen, but could do nothing to help. When the musher did arrive on the scene, the person instantly planted the snow hooks and ran up to the musher on the ground, asking, "Can you hear me? Are you all right?"

"I can hear you," Detective Murphy said, getting up from the snow. The fellow musher looked shocked before Mack went on to explain, saying, "I'm wearing a bullet proof vest because I'm a detective for the Fairbanks Police Department. The person who did this has already killed once, so I'll have to ask you to stay behind me. I don't want anyone else to get shot."

"Okay, I'll go ahead and rest my team here for a while."

"Thank you." Mack left the area on dog sled, still in pursuit of the perpetrator so that they might catch the killer ahead of them. When she finally did catch up to the murdering musher once again, she took no chances that he might react violently towards her so she quietly snuck around the area, climbing to an elevated area.

He put up a tent to rest, believing that he had a little room to relax before running away again. Once he was securely inside the tent, Mack snuck over to where he was and took his team away while he was sleeping. Taking them over by her team, they were hidden out of eyesight but not entirely out of mind. Detective Murphy returned to the tent and said, "Freeze! Come out of the tent with your hands up!"

The person came out, fired a shot to her chest and sprinted to where his team wasn't. Mack tackled the suspect to the ground, cuffing him as she said, "You're under arrest for the assault of an officer and if worst comes to worst, you'll be arrested for murder. You have the right to remain silent. You have the right to an attorney and if you can't afford an attorney, one will be appointed for you in a court of law."

"You can't arrest me for murder because I killed a Canadian citizen."

"You forget that it was on American soil that you murdered him and that makes this case under the jurisdiction of the IIA."

"What's that?" the culprit asked.

"An organization that you will get very well acquainted with in the next several days," Mack assured him.

"Who are you?"

"Who I am doesn't matter. Let me just remind you that you have the right to remain silent," Detective Murphy said before she made a phone call to Detective Tyler Clarke once again.

He answered the phone, saying, "Hello, this is Detective Clarke speaking. How might I help you?"

"Hey Tyler, I think that I'll help you. I have the suspect in custody for assault on an officer."

"Did you get shot again?"

"Well, yes and no. I was shot; however, I was wearing my bullet-proof vest so none of the bullets made contact with my actual body. We're not far from a checkpoint so I'll meet you there. By the way, I told a musher behind me not to pass me because of the violent nature of the suspect."

"All right, we'll make sure that they know that they can pass you now."

"Thanks, I'll meet you at the checkpoint then."

"Sounds good, I'll see you later, Mack."

About thirty minutes later, Detective Murphy came into the checkpoint with two teams of dogs. "Hi. I'm Mackenzie Murphy checking in."

"Are you going to stay for a while?"

"Yes and this is Martin Gruber. He is scratching from the race and on that note; I need to speak with the race officials."

"Okay, from the way it sounds, whatever you have to say must be important."

"Oh believe me, it is very important and it could possibly be history making, in fact."

"Okay, bed down and take care of your dogs over there. I'll make sure that the race officials will be right with you."

"Thanks." Mackenzie took her team and the other team, belonging to the arrested culprit, over to the area indicated in order to take care of the dogs. As an added security measure, Mack knocked the suspect out before she went about the task of feeding as best as she possibly could. She had just finished feeding and watering both teams when a group of race officials came over.

"Hi, you're Mackenzie Murphy, is that correct?"

"Yes, I am."

"We heard that you wished to speak with us?"

"Yes, I did. I believe that you've heard from a certain Detective Tyler Clarke, is that right?"

"Yes."

"Good then I should inform you that the person responsible has been arrested. That is why I came in with two dog sled teams and the musher, Martin Gruber in one of the sled baskets. Also, Detective Clarke and another person will come for this musher here sometime in the next hour or so."

"Okay, how has this person been arrested for an international incident, because it doesn't seem like you would have jurisdiction on this matter?"

"I arrested Martin Gruber for assault on an officer then I'll hand him over to the IIA for the murder charge, dropping the assault charge when it comes to that."

"What officer? Who was the officer that he assaulted for which he is being arrested?"

"That would be Detective Mackenzie Lynn Murphy of the Fairbanks Police Department."

"You're a detective from the Fairbanks Police Department?"

"Yes I am. I don't particularly care to make that knowledge known while I'm not on duty, but in this case, it's on a need-to-know basis. I've already been shot three times today and I don't particularly care to have others trying to do the same thing to me today or any other day."

Just then, Detective Clarke arrived on scene with David Danner; He took the suspect into the custody of the International Investigators' Agency. The suspect was conscious again as they arrested him and the race officials spoke with Detective Clarke as Mack went back to her dog sled team. She let her team rest for a while longer before she continued on down the Iditarod Trail, but her problems were far from being over. In fact, the problems were just beginning for Detective Mackenzie Murphy.

Mack headed out from the checkpoint and went soundly for quite a while. At least she was until they were coming around Old Woman Mountain. A moose came out of seemingly nowhere and hit the sled which caused the snow hooks to come out as Mackenzie went rolling away from the sled, hitting branches and small trees as she went. It wasn't until she finally hit a tree that she was able to come to a halt.

She heard a resounding "crack" and knew with almost absolute certainty that her leg was broken. She crawled back to the general area where the sled was. It took every ounce of determination she had in order to get back up to the sled and her dogs.

Thankfully, the moose had left and had not continued trying to attack the sled or team of dogs. Taking a couple of pain pills, Mackenzie Murphy pressed down on the brake as she got the snow hooks pulled from their firm entrenchment in the snow. She made it down the trail and stopped nearby a dog sled team that was stopped. A hideous red trail led away from the sled into the woods, prompting Mack to snack her team (where she would give them a chopped piece of meat that could be fish, chicken skins, beaver, lamb or anything to help with all the calories that the sled dogs consumed), and follow the crimson red staining. It turned out to be that there was a rabbit that had been mauled by an animal and drug off. Mack was on her way back when she stumbled onto another mystery.

She tripped over something and looked back to see a hand revealed from the snow's whiteness. She was instantly on the phone with Detective Clarke and her sentence was cut short when she was hit over the head and the phone call was hung up by the attacker.

Instantly knowing that something was wrong, Detective Clarke tracked the team's GPS, a relatively new addition to the sport of mushing, and they arrived on a scene that had no other team or musher in sight with no sign of Detective Murphy in view. Mack's team was still resting, but it was apparent that there was foul play involved with her disappearance. This was only about the thousandth time, figuratively speaking, that Mack managed to go missing.

As Mack woke up, she was in a cave, bound with a fire going nearby, and there was no one in sight. Putting her hands near the heat, the flames caught flamboyantly on fire, using the rope as fuel. She put the fire out once she felt that the rope on her wrists was giving way though it was also burning into her skin. The rope had weakened enough that she broke free from the bounds that held her hands and she ended up untying the bounds on her feet.

Her next thought was to escape from the cave; however, instead, she hid behind a large rock after grabbing some food that just happened to be beef jerky. Mack didn't have long to wait before someone entered into the cave or cavern, as you could call it, saying several curse words that came to mind. As he turned to leave, she hit him over the head with a small rock. When he came to, the situation had been reversed and he was the person in cuffs making him ask, "How'd you escape?"

"Does it really matter, Jordan Wes? I believe that's what your name is." Mackenzie coolly replied with his wallet in her hands as she sat comfortably chewing on jerky with the leg that had been broken, lying out with a splint.

After looking her over, he asked, "Who are you or what are you?"

"Who I am doesn't matter. I'm Mackenzie Murphy and, right now I'm just mad which means that I'm a maniac." Getting a log, or rather a stick to use as a cane, Detective Murphy went outside the cave for a while, in order to leave the man contemplating the situation and to look for some mode of transportation. She happened to notice a dog sled team that seemed as though it belonged to another Iditarod musher. It was then that she remembered a musher who had been friends with Martin Gruber. That was when she made the decision to take her prisoner back towards the direction that her dog sled team had been left.

After all their supplies had been loaded up, Mack placed Jordan Wes into the sled basket by gun point before she knocked him out again. Once she was back to her team, she noticed that there was evidence of activity; however, there was no one around. Again, she hooked up the two dog sled teams together and headed down the trail towards Unalakleet, the next checkpoint.

Little did she know, Detective Tyler Clarke arrived onto the scene where the dog sled had been and watched as the dog sled team disappeared into a barely distinguishable dot in the distance, powerless to do anything about the current situation. He had rushed to see that the team had left with David Danner right with him because they had heard the chorus of dogs as they left. They were unable to do anything about it except that whoever had the sled would make it to the next checkpoint in one piece so that justice could be done. That person was Detective Murphy and, running on only a few hours of sleep, she started up the trail thinking that every shadow was going to harm her with criminals lurking with guns. It was not long after they started up the trail that a storm blew in without any warning or hint of what was to come.

Following the trail markers, Mack ended up getting lost and she was surrounded by a wall of white-out snow conditions with only a wall of white that was stretched all around her. Through the whiteness, a man with a Pulaski in one hand and a chainsaw in the other led the team back to the trail. Considering the encounter as a hallucination with a certain amount of luck, Detective Murphy continued down the trail towards the next checkpoint that was waiting ahead of them. As she went along, music came to the front of her thoughts once she started to become more aware of her pain again. If only her day could be done with then maybe rest could finally come.

She arrived at the next checkpoint and, barely five minutes later, Jordan Wes attempted to escape as Detective Clarke and David Danner of the International Investigators' Agency (the IIA), were walking towards them. Mack tackled Jordan Wes to the ground, but not before the younger IIA agent, David Danner, fired off a shot from the hip in the general vicinity of the suspect. The bullet barely missed Detective Murphy by her knee. She ended up tripping instead; sending a jolt of pain that made her clench her teeth as tears welled up in her eyes from the pain in her broken leg.

Both men were on the scene as Detective Clarke directed David Danner to tend to the suspect as he looked after his former partner, who lay injured on the ground with her broken leg. With genuine concern, Detective

Clarke asked, "Mack, are you all right? You got that, Mackenzie?"

"Yes, but don't call me Mackenzie. I need to see my team first before anything else. I don't care what happens to me, I just want my team to be taken care of," Detective Murphy said even though it was obvious that she was in quite a bit of pain, but, regardless, there was no objecting with her as Mack tended to her dogs on her own two feet. After she was done, all the braveness and sheer resolve was replaced by a few tears in her eyes as she was supported by Detective Clarke and led away to receive medical attention.

The medical clinic took one look at her injuries and had an assistant go get the race officials. Once there, the general consensus of everyone was that Mackenzie Murphy needed more medical attention than what could be provided by facilities at that checkpoint due to possible damage in the leg that was broken. It was determined that Mack should be flown to Anchorage, Alaska where there were better facilities and she was withdrawn from the race.

The race committee accepted Detective Clarke's proposal to test the dogs and allow him to take them back once they were all cleared. Once Mack was at the Anchorage hospital, one of the nurses recognized her and had Mack get medical attention within minutes without having to ask insurance questions.

After everything was done and she was resting, Detective Murphy started having a dream that combined dog sledding and youth conservation work with some random activities (like basketball and five gallon wrestling) coming and going throughout her dreams. With such an interesting dream, Mack could only blame it on the medication before she woke up from the pain to see that there was the Fairbanks Police Department's chief of police and a forest ranger waiting for her to wake up.

Once the chief saw, from behind his newspaper, that Mackenzie was awake, he said, "Detective Murphy, we have a case for you that you're going to be provided accommodations for on the account of your injury. You won't and don't have anything to worry about when accepting this case." Mack nodded as she knew with an ever-increasing certainty and realization that crime never rests, not even for one second. Crime was just one of those things that would always be present in society, no matter what or who was involved. For the time-being, Mack just laid back, somewhat listening to the details of the case before sleep once again came to the detective.

CASE 24 ACTIVITIES

CRITICAL THINKING:

This case revolves around the world of mushing (also known as dog sledding) since it takes place during the Iditarod Trail Dog Sled Race. There are many different races than just the Iditarod, despite the fact that the Iditarod is the most well-known. What are a few of the different dog sled races? There are a few different types of dog sledding such as sprint and long-distance. What are the different types of dog sledding? There are different types of harnesses and gang lines that are used for mushing; what are some examples? Write a paper on mushing (dog sledding) including the questions posed in this critical thinking activity.

REVIEW QUESTIONS:

1) How is case jurisdiction determined between agencies when regarding murder? Which agency received the jurisdiction in this case?

2) What mistake did the culprit make? Why did this mistake help Detective Murphy eventually assist with the arrest?

3) How do you think Detective Murphy put the two sleds together once she had the culprit in order to take the teams into the checkpoint?

4) What mistake did Detective Clarke's IIA partner make when the culprit was escaping?

VOCABULARY:

Define and use in a sentence based on the definition for the word.

Untainted-

_____

Improvised-

_____

Perpetrator-

_____

VOCABULARY REVIEW:

Unscramble the word using the clues given and and write down a synonym of the word.

Eerzldivpu-Punished

_____

CASE 25:
TRIPLE THE TRICKS

Detective Murphy was riding in a plane from Alaska bound towards her next case with Forest Ranger J. Hankie from one of the ranger districts in Oregon. Pain was evident on her face as she looked out the window of the plane. A recent case, that was unofficially considered hers, had resulted in her current position because she had solved a case while running in the Iditarod Trail Dog Sled Race. Detective Murphy wasn't able to finish the Iditarod race, however, under the circumstances involved, but there was always next year. The fact that there was always next year just made her even more determined to finish the Iditarod next year.

It was while she was thinking that she had a feeling that they'd forgotten something pertaining to her luggage and tent. Her suspicions were confirmed when they landed. The bag which had her tent poles in it was still in Alaska. She knew then that she would have to use some ingenuity in order to go in the back country to solve a case.

They arrived very late into the camp where the crime had taken place. Making her tent lean-to in the dark wasn't much fun, but, despite the circumstances, Mack just had to laugh at the fact that the tent almost flew away. That hysteria probably originated more from dehydration though.

Waking up before the camp was up; the stars in the sky were jewels to a jeweler's eye. Each star was a sparkling gem with its glorious luster. However, it was just being awake that was all that Mack could muster. She didn't even know the case yet, but Mack wanted to be returning home to Alaska already. At least, she wanted to until she was introduced to the crime scene by Forest Ranger J. Hankie and one of the leaders of the group.

The case involved a senator's son from Montana while they were in Oregon and one of the other group members was there on a work visa from some foreign country that Mack couldn't remember at the moment. Due to her association with both her father and the International Investigators' Agency (IIA), it seemed that she was the obvious choice for such a case like this. How was the victim murdered, you might ask yourself? That was part of the mystery; that was also the beauty of the case. The other investigators were under the assumption that the remains were human, but in this case, they were not and it prompted Mack to go for a walk-about in order to find someone who was missing. That was when she found the missing member of the group and brought him back. When the missing corps member was brought back, Mackenzie was asked, "Who's that then if not James Alderson?" They said, indicating towards the mistaken remains.

"That would be James' idea of a cover-up in order to hide until he was able to get safely away without anyone realizing that he was actually alive. There's a deer here with a couple of squirrels and a rabbit, but needless to say, all of these animals have been mauled in order to give it the appearance of a mauled corpse," Mack explained.

Without any other hideous details or explanation, the corps member was fired. However, little did Mack know that there was a far greater murderer out there than any practical jokester trying to be invisible. This simple fact was made evident when they were coming back off of the trail and had to rest for a few minutes. When they returned from their rest, one of the pack horses was missing and there was a blood trail not five feet away, leading away into the woods.

Mack followed the trail with a pistol at the ready and. . .the next thing she knew, she was at the beach not far from a lighthouse with Detective Clarke standing above her. As he stood there, he saw her eyes open and Detective Clarke said, "Hey Mack, welcome back to the world of the living. Are you all right?"

"Where am I and how did I get here?"

"You don't remember?"

"No, I don't. Should I remember?"

"Yes, you should because you've just solved three cases in a week. What's the last thing that you remember?"

"I was in Oregon on my way back from a back country case when one of our pack horses was missing with a blood trail leading into woods prompting me to follow it. That's the last thing I remember until just now, waking up on the beach."

"You don't remember anything from that time until waking up just now? I've heard of ridiculous, but how could you possibly lose six days while still being able to solve two cases?"

"I honestly don't know. Do you know what happened to me?"

"No, but we'll find out together, no matter what that might be," he assured her.

"Thanks, I really appreciate it," Mack said just before she was lifted up by Detective Clarke with her many injuries and her rationalizing mind running wild with unanswered questions.

It was in the pursuit of answers for those questions that led the duo to meet up with Ranger Hankie. Immediately, once they were out of the vehicle, the forest ranger said, "Hey there, Detective Murphy, how's your injury coming along?"

"It should be coming along great, but I don't remember the past six days since I went into the woods following the trail of blood once we discovered that one of the pack horses was missing. I don't know exactly what I did, but it was as though I was there, however, at the same time, I was not there since I don't remember."

"Did Detective Murphy experience a traumatic experience because that could explain this?" Ranger Hankie asked.

"Not that I know of, but it is possible that Mack lost those six days as the result of a previous injury. She has suffered amnesia a couple of times in the past, I believe, but nothing like this where she has lost six days." Tyler responded.

"Okay guys, can we leave all hypotheses here and do some actual investigating into what happened?"

"All right, Detective Murphy, I'll start off with what I know: you went into the woods and returned with a man named Mr. R. Smith, but he just went by Smith. We took the pack horses to his cabin and pasture before we were invited into his cabin. Basically the entire time that we were there in the cabin, Mr. Smith sat on a sofa petting his Siamese Tabby cat named Sully as he told us a description of the culprit. We ended up having two of the packers put up the horses and mules before we continued on and that is when you were separated from us for a half an hour before you turned up talking to a couple of fishermen at the river."

Ranger Hankie paused and Mack took that opportunity to say, "We should start by interviewing Mr. Smith and start from the beginning." Both of the men consented to that action and it wasn't too long afterwards that they were on their way to Mr. Smith's cabin. Once there, they received a menacing stare as he sat on the porch in a rocking chair petting his cat, Sully.

As they got closer, he yelled out, "Stay where you are! Who are you?"

"I'm Detective Murphy. I met you about six days ago, but I don't ever remember meeting you before now," Mack replied.

"Now I remember. That was two days before the Chicago Bulls played. I watched, well heard, the game over the television. There was too much interference with the antenna to do anything else. Come on in, I have the air conditioning running and it's pretty hot out here."

"Do you mind me asking what you were doing outside on the porch when you have a nice and cool house inside?"

"It's because of Sully and the fact that he needs a sprinkling of sunshine to keep him spectacular. At least, that's what the vet's orders were," Smith said with the hint of a smile and even Mack had a slight smile as they all went inside Smith's cabin in order to uncover some truth.

As Smith listened to the forest ranger relate Mack's problem with amnesia, he stroked Sully with a silent smile. When he finally spoke, Smith said, "I've heard this happen only once before in my thirteen years of living here and that was because of a very rare and uncommon plant known as the arborous gencigorpus, I believe. I just call it the absent-minded plant or the absent-minded professor's plant because of the effect it has on a person."

Smith pulled out a book and flipped it open to an article about the problem. The information fit the condition except the question still remained: what had happened to Mack during the past six days? That question was combined with the question: how did Detective Murphy even solve two cases while being affected by such an unheard of plant? When asked about the local fishermen that Mack had talked with, Mr. Swenson and Mr. Maurine, Mr. Smith explained that they were two foreigners who have been living in the region for a year and a half. They were retired from their former jobs so they went fishing every day.

It was because of this information that the trio left from Mr. Smith's cabin to a river where they met up with Mr. Swenson as he was fishing. He had just barely netted a silver trout, sparkling underneath the sunshine, when they arrived on the riverbank. Mr. Swenson came up with his prize, placing the trout in a brown basket with a leather clasp.

Mr. Swenson turned towards them after that and immediately struck up a conversation with Detective Murphy in French while the other two people present could only make out a word here and there. Once the conversation was over, Mr. Swenson turned back to his fishing pole while Mack explained to Detective Clarke and Ranger Hankie what the conversation was about. They were able to find out more particulars of her disappearance because the fisherman had informed her of a man living in a shack along the river who would know anything about anyone on the shore or on the river anywhere around his general area.

Their next step was to go to the shack on the river which gave Ranger Hankie more time to relate the course of events before they reached yet another place of possibilities to solve Mack's memory problem.

Apparently, according to Ranger Hankie, this shack was not mentioned previously in their investigation; however, it wasn't too long after talking with the fisherman that Mack had uncovered what had happened to the pack horse, quite by accident of course. The horse was found by a grandmotherly old lady living at a little cottage in the woods, bringing to life the old song that had the lyrics: 'over the river and through the woods to grandmother's house we go'. The old lady's house was over the river and through the woods with the resemblance of last year's garden from which the horse had eaten.

It was now that Mack was knowledgeable about what had actually happened. They still went to the shack by the river to see what additional information could be given to them. Unfortunately for Mack, the instant they got in the shack, a flood of memories came rushing back of other people's troubles and the ripple effect that those memories had.

It was apparent that there was illegal paraphernalia in the residence, however, there are times that you have to just let things go in order to learn and live. This was one of those instances because if Detective Murphy had taken the resident, Billy Jo Daniels, to jail, Mr. Daniels wouldn't have told them anything regarding their investigation.

The memories still lingered, but it was for the greater good of any investigation that a detective's rationalizing, detail-orientated mind wasn't combined with any personal problems. Mack stopped thinking of the issues and just the problem that faced her currently. It was as though it was a puzzle that could only be solved by relying on her deduction about what pieces went where. It was like an exercise that she had done as a teenager, completing a puzzle blind-folded with every piece lined up perfectly by deduction rather than by sight.

Despite all the case's complexity, combined with frustration for the detective, certain facts were revealed in the conversation with Billy Jo Daniels. Detective Clarke, Ranger Hankie and Detective Murphy learned more information based on the fact that Jo had seen another teenager helping the person responsible for putting the pack horse in the old lady's garden. This was after they sold a deer to a restaurant in town.

It was another example of a prankster's practical joke combined with the effort to get away with illegal and incorrigible acts in order to tempt trouble. The new information led to the arrest of Thomas Lewis as an accomplice to the previous arrest of Adam Hays.

When Thomas was brought in, it was just about five o'clock, prompting the three people who had now found answers about one investigation, to have dinner at a café not far from the sheriff's office. While there, Ranger Hankie thanked them for all they had done before glancing at his watch and taking his leave to get some more things done before bed.

After his departure, Detective Clarke briefed Mackenzie on the final case that took place at an Arizona beach, not far from Port Orford, Oregon. Detective Clarke briefed her by saying, "Hey Mack, along the line of your current amnesia, we're down to the last case and the last four days involved with what I consider to be confusion with this case. It all started when we were called into the case because of some misdirection and miscommunication, on part of the local police department. The reason that I was called into the case was because of the dual citizenship of a few suspects. Among those suspects was a Canadian-American and a German-American and it was these two who were two of the ten primary suspects. During this time, you were put undercover with a very unbelievable cover-story while me and my partner, Jacob "Jake" Orison tried to solve the case." Detective Clarke said all that before pausing to drink some water from the glass provided at the café while Mack continued to listen attentively with a cup of coffee in her hand.

It was during this pause that they were interrupted by a little girl in pigtails in her hair and the girl's mother who had recognized her as a previous teacher for the elementary school in Fairbanks, Alaska on Chilly Lane. It was during the conversation that Mack realized something startling namely that her fame as a detective had spread across the Northwest and Alaska. Beforehand, it had only been her father's fame that had always preceded Mackenzie so it was a strange concept actually to consider her own fame rather than that of her father. It wasn't long after that epiphany, so to speak, that the mother and daughter left them with the daughter's pigtails and ribbons dancing during their departure as the little girl skipped along.

Once gone, Detective Clarke was prompted to continue the briefing by saying, "For time-conservation or time-management, you might say, I think that it would be a better use of our time if we just review the case file." Detective Clarke said with a smile.

Detective Murphy responded to by saying, "That's the best idea that you've had all day, but I also need to do some research so I guess that the question I'm trying to ask is: will we be able to access the case file online? If we are able to then I need to know so I can get out my laptop."

Detective Clarke had to think about that question for a bit before he finally answered, "I believe that you'll be able to access it online, but don't count on it. I suggest that we wait until tomorrow to work on it so that camp could be set up tonight at a campground not far from here."

Mack got a to-go mug for her coffee before she said, "Okay."

Heading to the waiting vehicle, Mack kept having a bad feeling that wouldn't go away. At the last possible moment, she noticed the bomb underneath the undercarriage of the vehicle with thirteen seconds on it. Practically throwing Detective Clarke out of harm's way, Detective Murphy was barely able to take cover from the blast behind a stone monument that spared her life. Looking out from behind the monument, Mack caught a glimpse of a person's face as they fled the scene of the explosion. Despite the briefness of the encounter, Mack recognized the person from somewhere, but she just couldn't remember where. It was only about a minute before an ambulance arrived on the scene. In that time, Detective Clarke came up to her and asked, "What just happened?"

"Our vehicle exploded and my coffee got spilled so now I'm mad. Is there anyone else?" Mack said and without any further hesitation, she went to see if there were any other possible victims from the explosion.

That was when the paramedics showed up and made both of the detectives sit down. It was also when they bandaged a cut on Detective Clarke's head before clearing both detectives to go home and rest. There was only one problem with those instructions and that was the fact that they were away from home with only one sleeping bag and tent at a different location. Since Mack's possessions were at the sheriff's department, the detectives went there in a taxi in order to find out some additional information. Once there at the station, Detective Clarke explained the situation while Mack got a cup of coffee. All the while,

Mack tried fervently to remember where she recognized that person before it all came back to her.

A few cases back, Detective Murphy and Detective Clarke had gone to California in order to help with a case there and they had ended up arresting a Californian teen by the name of Parker Cooley. One of the other teens involved with that situation had an older brother who was in the military, with explosives experience. How did Mack know this? It was all because of a probation officer's review for parole prompted by some good behavior. Detective Murphy had met with both the probation officer and the parole-worthy person. In the end, the decision had been made to deny parole and Mack received a threatening letter afterwards that only said, WATCH YOUR BACK! It wasn't considered that much of a threat and time decreased the potency, so to speak, of the threat.

As Mack came back with her cup of coffee, coincidentally, she came across another detective who slipped his cell phone number into her pocket. Mackenzie didn't acknowledge the fact that she clearly outclassed him and the fact that he was unsuccessful in achieving his goal without her knowledge.

Detective Clarke, meanwhile, had managed to get some assistance by receiving an offer to stay with the chief and his family until they found another vehicle to transport them to their next destination. Of course, given their situation, the two detectives couldn't refuse such a generous offer from the chief of police, so they ended up going to a five bedroom, three bathroom house up a road surrounded by blossoming trees.

The quietness of the entire situation made Detective Mack Murphy glad that everything worked out for the better. In fact, an overwhelming sense of calm and community overcame her. The only draw-back was the fact that Detectives Clarke and Murphy had to wait until the chief said a blessing and made introductions before the hungry detectives could eat the delicious dinner prepared, but even that wasn't that bad of a draw-back.

After dinner, Mack got onto the computer and looked up the case file with brief flashes of memory being prompted by the description of the case. Based on the book that Mr. Smith had provided for their use while they had been at his cabin, she should be able to regain bits and pieces of her memory over the next month so that she'd have complete remembrance of all the events that had transpired after a month's time.

With clarity giving her a sense of calm, Mackenzie Murphy ended up falling asleep on a couch, oblivious to anything until five-thirty when she woke up and got some coffee going, almost immediately.

Sitting down at her packs, she pulled out the laptop and went back over the case about yet another trickster who created a large explosion before going missing to put all suspicion towards someone else. In the end, Detective Murphy had found some of this information out by another member of the organization in whom the missing person had confided. Most people would have the term 'snitch' come directly to mind, to only name one derogatory term. However, that person didn't give up any information intentionally. Detective Mackenzie Murphy, even while under the effects of arborous gencigorpus, was able to deduce the untruth and location of the entire situation.

What ended up happening was that Mack found a cave with the missing suspect inside. She notified Detective Clarke and his temporary partner, Jake Orison, of that information. Leaving a red bandana tied to a root at the entrance, Mack ended up finding an alternate exit. When Detective Tyler Clarke and Detective Jake Orison (if he could be considered a detective) entered into the cave from the entrance with the red bandana, it only acted as a catalyst to force the suspect out of the alternate exit where Mack was waiting. Struggling, a shot was fired into the air before Detective Murphy was hit by the suspect and sent off of the cliffs and into the ocean.

Jake Orison ended up arresting the stunned suspect while Detective Clarke, without hesitation or thought to the contrary, jumped off the cliff into the ocean below to save the detective who was previously his partner, Mackenzie Murphy. Dragging her back to shore, he immediately began CPR with mouth-to-mouth. Once Mack sputtered out salt-water, it was obvious that she would live.

However, there was one more unresolved issue before Mack could go back to her cabin in Alaska. That one last thing was to solve the explosion incident involving their vehicle in Oregon. Solving that case required the use of technology without being present on the crime scene. Accessing the newly-built in monitoring system by her laptop, there was a positive identification by the computer of who the suspect was and it turned out to be Jack "Steve" Johnson, the older brother of John Lee Johnson. Shortly after she found this information, at seven twenty-five, Detective Clarke woke up as Mack was pouring a second cup of coffee for her own consumption. Mack informed Detective Clarke of the information that she had acquired through her research on the laptop into the explosive incident that they had experienced.

When the chief of police woke up at seven thirty, they all drove to the station, making only one stop along the way to the station and that was at a donut shop for two or three dozen variety donuts. Among those donuts were the crème-filled long-johns, apple fritters, raspberry-filled powdered donuts, and apple-filled donuts, just a few of the choices that were within the confines of the donut boxes. Once at the station, Mack wiped off the remnants of the donut she had for breakfast from her face before the seriousness of the situation returned.

Two detectives were put on the case and both Detective Clarke and Detective Murphy gave their statements before they were allowed to be driven to the airport in order to catch a plane to Alaska. Asleep almost the instant the airplane took off, Mack could only dream and think of the forty-ninth state. Among those dreams was the dream of running behind a dog sled through the woods of the mountains that they called home. Snow fell softly from the sky as the sled slid on the snow towards the sunrise before her. The sunrise reminded her of the aurora borealis that would transform the scene into one with the mountains and velvety black night sky. It would be underneath the flashing and flickering lights that wolves ran endlessly in the pursuit of the answers and nourishment that could not be obtained once they died.

Still, they ran towards the stars, striving forwards to their desires and dreams as though they were chasing buffalo until the scene turned to the darkness that was considered absolute sleep with no disruptions during the long flight home.

CASE 25 ACTIVITIES:

CRITICAL THINKING:

In this case, Detective Murphy was forced to retrace her steps from the past few days in order to find out what had happened. This technique for finding out what happened is a part of police work. How can you apply this technique to your life to find something that you are missing? How effective is this technique? Write a paragraph regarding retracing your steps in order to locate something you lost.

REVIEW QUESTIONS:

1) What state did the first case, in Case 25: Triple the Tricks, take place? Where exactly is that location on a map?

2) How does Detective Murphy succeed in finding out about the information that she has missed? Why did she need to find out about it?

3) What was the name of the plant that had affected Detective Murphy in such a memory matter?

4) What was the realization for Mack that came about at the café where Detective Clarke was relating the events that had taken place? Why was this realization important to Detective Murphy? How do you think that realization made Mack feel?

VOCABULARY:

Define and use in a sentence based on the definition for the word.

Hysteria-

_____

Incorrigible-

_____

Transpired-

_____

Derogatory-

_____

Coincidentally-

_____

VOCABULARY REVIEW:

 Unscramble the word and write down the word's definition.

oeethcnr- intelligible; comprehensible

_____

CASE 26:
FRIEND OR FOE

Detective Mackenzie Murphy woke up with such a headache and a really bad feeling that something was wrong. She went into a bathroom and ended up face-to-face with herself looking into a mirror with blood covering her face and hands. Only a little of it was her own by the extent of the blood, prompting her to grow suspicious of the situation and look for some answers. However, it ended up exactly as Mack had deduced from the moment at the mirror. She found a corpse on the ground and ended up calling the cops.

Although, Detective Mackenzie Murphy would have never expected to be arrested without being read any of her rights, she was brought into the Fairbanks Police Department and the chief of police was brought to her cell within moments of being informed that Mack had been arrested for murder. In the time that it took for everything to happen, from the moment that Mack Murphy was arrested up until the chief of police showed up, she tried to recall the order of events.

All she was successful in remembering was coming home after spending some time with a friend of hers. She had gone to bed, falling asleep almost instantly without any other recollection until she woke up to the discovered occurrences. When the chief appeared, he could only say, "Mack, I'm not going to tell you how bad this looks right now because you already know, being a detective such as yourself right now. Your case is going to the state and it's that plain and simple. Do you have anything that you would like to say to me as your friend rather than your chief?"

Mack looked at him with a certain amount of regret at the fact that she couldn't remember what had happened before she said, "Just call in some of my friends to help. I'm not going to name any names, but just call in my friends and anyone else you can think of who would be able and willing to help. I just don't remember what happened to me so, as much as I hate to admit it, I need help because I'm anything but a murderer."

The chief nodded his head and said, "I'll see what I can do," before he left to to go to his office, where a couple of tears formed in his eyes. Wiping the tears, the chief called several people in a really short time to come help with the murder suspect, Mackenzie Lynn Murphy. When all of the calls for assistance had been made, the chief made the one phone call to the Alaska State Police. He really wished that circumstances such as those currently facing them didn't have to happen.

Back in her cell, Detective Mack Murphy could only think and reflect, looking and searching fervently for any shred of remembrance that could give her the peace of mind that she needed by knowing without a doubt that she was innocent. However, until that time, Mack was surrounded by a shadow of unknowing and uncertainty. It was apparent at that time, that without knowledge of a previous event; she and the rest of the world would have to face the possibility of failure.

Detective Tyler Luke Clarke, meanwhile, had been sitting at his desk when another International Investigatory Agency (IIA) Agent approached him with the simple question of who his previous partner had been. Thinking nothing of the question, Detective Clarke replied by saying, "My previous partner was Detective Mackenzie Murphy."

The person who asked, handed him a file saying, "Some partner or previous partner because Detective Mackenzie Murphy was arrested for murder. It might become an international incident depending on what comes up on the victim's records. Anyway, Agent Clarke, here's the file."

"Thank you."

"You're welcome." Detective Clarke opened the file with some pages that were still warm inside it. Looking it over, it looked as though Mackenzie Murphy was guilty, but how could she be? He had been her partner, and while he had to admit that she was relatively insane, there was no way that she could be the murderer in this case, or was there?

Thinking back on all the things that they'd done and all the cases that they'd solved, the only time that Detective Clarke had even questioned Mack's ability to murder was on Case 18: Crystal Mountain Madness. During that instance, Mackenzie had proven herself as a detective and not as a murderer because of the fact that she wasn't that mad to the point of committing murder. Knowing this, he knew that Mackenzie wouldn't murder and that the normally independent detective needed help for once in her life.

Knowing this, the detective's report was left unfinished as Detective Tyler Clarke got on his phone for the next half an hour, calling friends that would be able to help. After that, Detective Clarke called the Alaska State Police and the Fairbanks Police Department in order to find out more information about what was going on regarding Detective Mackenzie Murphy's arrest and case. It was in this way that he learned that the case had just turned into an international incident so that it was going to the IIA.

The Chief Inspector came to Detective Clarke and said, "Agent or Detective Clarke, whichever you prefer to be called, I need to see you in my office right now."

"Yes, Chief, be right there." Detective Clarke responded as he followed the chief Inspector into his office.

The chief spoke seriously, closing the door and shutting the blinds behind their entrance, saying, "Have a seat, Tyler Clarke." Once Detective Clarke had complied with the request, the chief went on to say, "Detective Clarke, I understand that you are aware of the fact that your previous partner's murder case has just turned into an international incident. Is that information correct?"

"Yes chief, I'm aware of that information."

"Good. I hate to do this to you, especially considering the circumstances that you are one of the best agents we have working for the IIA, but we're sending you out to the Sahara Desert. There's an international criminal in the area and I want you to arrest her. You'll have some help from some other IIA agents that will come after you set up a perimeter in order to provide ground support for their approach by air."

"Let me get this right, so I'll be going to the Sahara Desert in order to arrest an international criminal is that correct?"

"Yes it is."

"Another thing. Why did you just call the international criminal a her as though the criminal was a woman?"

"That's because the criminal is a woman."

"Really? Who might that be?"

"You will be going into the Sahara Desert in order to arrest Sonya Ramekin."

"I think I recognize the last name of that international criminal."

"You should, because Sonya's father and grandfathers were all wanted international criminals."

"Okay. I can see what you're wanting and why you want me to do it. If I remain here, I just might help with Mack's murder investigation which would hinder instead of help."

"Yes, that is the reason I'm putting you on this other case. Do you want to take on this case in the Sahara?"

"Yes, I'll take it on. Just let me know my travel itinerary and what the plan is for my help with this case."

"Okay, we can do that," the chief paused before he went on to lay out the plan and provide the necessary clarity on the situation where there had been none previously. Still, ever-present in the back of his mind, Detective Clarke couldn't stop wondering about his partner, since he still considered her as his partner, and what the outcome of the murder trial might be. Detective Clarke was just left to listen to what was scheduled for him. All Detective Clarke could do was wait and wonder.

Despite what Detective Clarke was going through, it was in support of Mackenzie Murphy that the president requested that the best of the best help represent the detective in question. In this case, however, the best of the best: Sofia Scoria, Vladimir Vorkordov, and Arnold Günter, wouldn't have been able to clear Mack's guilt had it not been for the undercover efforts of Joshua Murphy, Samantha Simmons (her dog sled handler), and Dr. Price (doctor whose life she had saved).

Knowing that Mackenzie wouldn't murder, they went undercover, playing the role of sleuths to locate the evidence that their friend, boss, or relative had not murdered. Samantha and Dr. Price served as the distraction and look out in obtaining such evidence. What they found was a discarded security video underneath the desk that showed what had happened. When they had found the security video footage, they took a photo of the location of it and put latex gloves on while handling and bagging it up. The important thing was the fact that in the footage, it showed Detective Murphy falling asleep and a couple of thieves entering in from the window.

Fighting over some item, one of the thieves stabbed the other thief repeatedly until movement from a door caused the guilty thief to flee out the window with nothing. Sleep-walking, Mack attempted to revive the victim, but the person didn't make it despite all of her attempts. Exhausted, Detective Murphy ended up falling back to sleep on the couch.

Providing it to the investigation, they submitted the footage to the police and to the best of the best investigators, who were put on the case, anonymously due to their connection to the case. It provided just enough circumstantial evidence that proved Detective Mackenzie Lynn Murphy was innocent.

There was only one question left to answer since Mack was proven innocent and that was: who did kill the victim if Mack didn't? Sure, they knew that this was the other thief; however, they didn't know the other thief's identity. That was when they checked surveillance footage at a gas station up the road out of curiosity and that provided the IIA the necessary photo in order to get a proper identification of the suspect.

It was shortly afterwards that the IIA arrested the suspect and took him into interrogation, reading him his rights in an international incident. Knowing his rights, the suspect broke down during interrogation, confessing to the murder with only a solitary tear to show the slightest amount of humanity. Still, there was no regret and it was obvious that the suspect, Aaron Allen, was the person responsible.

It was after this fact that the chief inspector of the IIA contacted the Fairbanks Police Department. Detective Mackenzie Murphy was still detained in a cell. Being cleared, the IIA informed the Fairbanks Police Department's Chief of Police that Detective Mack Murphy was not the murderer and that she was cleared of any and all charges. With obvious relief, the chief of police thanked the chief inspector for letting them know before he went to inform Detective Murphy.

Approaching the cell, he found Mack Murphy napping which prompted him to say, "Detective Mackenzie Murphy, wake up."

"What's the news, Chief?" Mack replied, getting up to her feet in anticipation.

The chief paused nervously before replying, "Mack, you're free. They found out what really happened and they ended up arresting Aaron Allen for the murder of Sylvester DeMoine."

"Thank you, Chief. Do my friends and family know yet?"

"Not yet, but I'm sure that you'll tell them."

"What about my previous partner, Detective Tyler Clarke? Does he know?"

"Not yet and there's something that you should know."

"What?"

"Detective Clarke is in the Sahara Desert for a case involving an international criminal," the chief explained.

"Okay, thank you. Does this all mean that I can get out of this cell now?"

"Yes, it does." Mackenzie was let out of her cell and she was allowed to regain her possessions before the chief wanted to talk with her. Entering into the chief's office, he returned Mack's pistol and badge to her, saying, "Mackenzie Murphy, in all my years, I've seen quite a few detectives turn bad, but I hope that you never have to lose your badge and be falsely accused of murder ever again. Is that understood, Detective?"

"Yes Chief. I don't want anything like this to happen to me again either. Once was enough to emphasize that point to me. I only wish that I could stay out of trouble sometimes because, as Detective Clarke says, I'm one of the luckiest of the unluckiest people that he knows."

"On that note, Mack, what is keeping you from joining the IIA? Your partner is there and I don't understand why you didn't go."

"Chief, I have a loyalty to Alaska and to Fairbanks. Yes, I have a loyalty to my partner; however, I have a greater loyalty to this department and town despite what anyone might think. Call me crazy if you like, but it was not an easy decision."

"No detective, it was a logical decision and that is a sweet and sour thing. It keeps you rational and detail-orientated. However, it prevents you from having fun sometimes because you don't go with your gut as much as you should. Despite that, Detective, your Murphy Madness is what makes you the best detective in the department and possibly in this state. I want you to take a week Mack. After that, you can come back to the cases and crime."

"All right, that sounds like a plan. If, for some strange reason, I need some more time, could I have it?"

"Yes, Mack, you have it if you need it. Just keep me updated because I don't need my best detective dying on me again," the chief said, emphasizing the word "again" because of the times that Mack was believed dead.

"How many times would that make it that I've died?"

"Once too many times, so don't die again."

"Okay, Chief. Thanks. I'm going to go home then."

"Go ahead, Mack. See you in a week, Detective." Mack nodded and left the Fairbanks Police Department to the parking lot where a vehicle was waiting for her. Heading home, while listening to the songs on the radio stations, she could only reminisce about her friends and what had just happened to her during that time in the cell.

Once she was at home, she fed her sled dogs, and all the while, she continued thinking of the detective currently in the Sahara Desert. Going to sleep, Detective Murphy crawled into the comforts of her comforter and dreams that awaited there within her relaxation. Dreaming of friends, Mack kept having the feeling that something was wrong. There was only one problem; she didn't know what was not right. What was worse was the fact that the feeling wouldn't go away, leaving Mack to wonder. . .what was wrong? What was WRONG? That was a question only to be answered by silence as it could not be answered. What could be answered was this: Detective Mackenzie Lynn Murphy was not a murderer, but in fact, a hero. It had been determined that Mack was a friend's friend rather than a foe's adversary in Case #26: Friend or Foe.

CASE 26 ACTIVITIES:

CRITICAL THINKING:

Name an instance where you were wrongly accused of something? How did it make you feel? Did that person believe you when you denied their accusation? What was that person's reaction when it turned out that you were correct and they were wrong? Write down what answers you've come up with and expound upon the topic regarding unjust accusation.

REVIEW QUESTIONS:

1) What would you do in a position where you couldn't remember anything and were accused of a crime that you didn't think that you could commit? How would that accusation make you feel?

2) Why do you think Detective Murphy would want to clear her name? What might her thought process have been when working to expel any doubt?

3) If you were in Detective Clarke's position where your previous partner was accused of murder, how would you feel? What actions would you take if you were in that position? How would they be different or similar to the action that Detective Clarke took or was forced to take?

4) What might the location that Detective Clarke is sent to tell you about the next case? Why would this bit of information be important to know?

VOCABULARY:

Define and use in a sentence based on the definition for the word.

Circumstantial-

_____

Humanity-

_____

VOCABULARY REVIEW:

Unscramble the word and write down the word's definition.

lryaict-Clearness

_____

eepnttmcloa-ponder

_____

Dtoouoxhrn- Unusual

_____

CASE 27:
SAHARA SANDS

Detective Mackenzie Murphy had entered into the Fairbanks Police Department to finish up a couple of reports. Sitting at her desk while staring off into space, she was thinking of fonder memories with all her friends and family, while Detective Murphy's computer stayed on the same sentence of the same report that she had been working on for the past twenty minutes. The phone rang and brought her back to reality. Clearing her mind of all distractions Mack answered the phone to stop its incessant noise. Detective Murphy didn't get the chance to respond because the person on the other end of the line began speaking instantly, saying, "Hi, we need Detective Mackenzie Murphy to come to the IIA at a location that will be provided at a later time. Just have Detective Murphy go to the Fairbanks Municipal Airport to take a flight to an unknown location. A packet of papers will be provided upon take off from the airport. Is that understood?"

"This is Detective Murphy speaking and I would like to know if I need any luggage or equipment."

"Just a carry-on if you want it, but travel light because we will provide most everything else once you arrive here. Does that sound acceptable to you?"

"Yes. In fact, I'll be there as soon as I possibly can."

"That sounds good detective. Thank you for your prompt response. Good-bye." Detective Murphy hung up the phone and closed down the computer before she grabbed a pack, telling the chief that the IIA wanted her assistance.

Leaving the Fairbanks Police Department, she drove to the Fairbanks Municipal Airport where she was met by an IIA representative, who just happened to be David Danner. He was a previous part-time partner of Detective Clarke who had helped and somewhat hindered while problems were presented during the insanity of the Iditarod Dog Sled Race. Despite everything that had happened, Detective Murphy greeted him warmly with an extraordinary amount of kindness, considering the fact that he had just about shot her when trying to hit a suspect. Still, she had a case to solve and if she could ensure that there were no hard feelings between them then it would be worthwhile, besides, Mack had too many enemies as it was, she didn't need any more.

Mack followed David Danner as they boarded a small four-person aircraft. The plane was filled with the pilot, co-pilot, David Danner, and Detective Mackenzie Murphy before it took off, soaring upwards into the blue sky above. Once they were in the air, David Danner pulled out a packet and handed it to Mack in order for her to look it over. Considering the fact that the pilot and co-pilot also worked for the IIA, Detective Murphy was free to talk about the situation that was about to be addressed . . . a situation regarding her previous partner Detective Clarke.

Two Days Earlier. . .

Detective Clarke was climbing over a sand dune in order to get in a better position to observe a known international criminal wanted for an international incident that they were investigating. Detective Clarke was going to help bring the criminal to justice by helping to provide ground support for the criminal's extraction. Detective Tyler Clarke ended up topping the sand dune only to see a rogue militant group attacking the area. He contacted the IIA on the radio before approaching closer to the camp. All that he remembered was going closer to the camp before he heard a crunch behind him and a patrol guard brought the butt of a gun down onto his head.

When he came to, he realized that there was a body on top of him. Throwing the corpse off, Detective Clarke ended up looking into the barrel of a gun with a lady at the other end of the barrel, holding it towards him. Venturing a guess, he queried, "Are you Sonya Ramekin?"

With a perplexed look, she asked, "Do I know you?"

"No you don't know me, but I know of you and your fame as an international criminal."

"Oh, that. Are you a friend or an adversary?"

"I'm whatever you want me to be, whether it is foe or friend."

"Were you involved with this attack?"

"No, I was not." Tyler truthfully denied.

"What are you? Are you an American CIA agent?"

"No, I work more internationally than that and you probably haven't heard of us yet."

"Well, you aren't married so you can be tortured for information or join our cause and fight for us even if it has to be at gun point. Men, bring him with us." At that,

Detective Clarke was pushed away at gunpoint towards an unknown destination.

Two Days Later. . .

Detective Mackenzie Murphy arrived at the (IIA) International Investigators Agency with her logical rationalizing mind contemplating the complexity of the situation. Detective Tyler Luke Clarke had been killed or captured in the Sahara Desert. In either instance, Tyler was MIA (missing in action) according to the IIA (International Investigators Agency).

That was when, after finding out additional information and knowledge about the unfortunate event, Detective Mack Murphy bought a round trip ticket to the Sahara desert, which meant going to Africa. She was dropped off alone by the military aircraft that she just so happened to be lucky enough to get a ride on and from then on, her country had plausible deniability of anything that went wrong with her unofficial rescue mission.

Dressing undercover as one of the nomadic people of the region, Mack ended up traveling with a caravan to the area where the international criminal, Sonya Ramekin, was reported to be at currently, since the last intelligence report that they had acquired. It was then that the real work started because Mack had to act as though she was a terrorist, or rather a criminal, in order to get anywhere near the international criminal and her captives. That was when her one year of drama during high school came in handy as Detective Murphy pretended, well, acted as though she was mute and somewhat more unintelligent than the average criminal or person. However, despite the obvious unintelligence of the character she was portraying, there was still a willingness to fight that trumped the lack of brains.

Detective Clarke, meanwhile, was being treated rather fairly, all things considered. Since his capture, Detective Clarke had gone with the criminals as a captive as they took him to an alternative base of operations that they had in the Sahara. Once there, even though he was confined, he was still fed three times a day. Rather than being tortured, Tyler had to have conversations with Sonya every day, who was intrigued by the American that had been captured. In one of the conversations, Sonya asked, "Do you have any romantic interests in America?"

"Yes, and heaven help those who stand in her way."

"Why? Your American women are thin and fragile, aren't they?"

Detective Clarke heard this and chuckled responding, "Some may be, but Mack is not one of those women."

"Mack? That sounds more like a man's name instead of a woman's." Sonya mocked.

"Her name is Mackenzie, but she goes by Mack."

"She must be some woman from the way that you speak of her."

"Oh, believe me, she is. I was engaged to her, but that was before I took on this job. Not this particular job, mind you, but by becoming what I am now. In doing so, I lost Mack and she just might be dead because of a murder charge while I'm stuck out in the Sahara desert."

"That sounds like a poorly written script or a sorry excuse for a romance novel. Are you telling me the truth?"

"Yes, I am and I'm glad that I'm not in your position right now because Mack won't stop or rest when and if she knows that I'm gone and lost in the Sahara...if she is still alive."

"Why's that? Is your Mack some kind of special forces soldier?"

"I wouldn't put it past her but no, the military doesn't permit women in combat situations like that, yet."

"That's unfortunate. From the way you speak of her, Mack must be one amazing woman. It almost makes me wish that I had someone like that working for me and I know how I can." Turning away from Detective Clarke, Sonya said to one of her leaders: "Tighten security and if you see an American woman or any American in general, I want you to capture them."

"Yes, Sonya, as you command."

"Put this American away, I've spent enough time on him today."

"Yes, Sonya." Someone said obediently and, as Detective Clarke was led away, Sonya Ramekin took a seat on a plush cushion, relaxing after her conversation. Little did she know that there was no need to tighten the security because Mack was already in their midst walking amongst the criminals and culprits of crimes committed.

Detective Murphy saw the tightening security measures and took it all in stride, formulating a plan to get both people, Detective Clarke and Sonya Ramekin, out of the area without too much blood shed if at all possible. It was upon the discovery of an aircraft in the area that a smile spread across her lips at the prospective plan. Everything was coming together for the rescuer and Mack found out additional information, waiting for the opportune moment at nightfall to put her plan into motion.

Once nightfall finally did come, the night was just perfect for what Mack had planned; sneaking into the main area where the prisoner was being held, not far from where Sonya Ramekin was. The best possible route was available to her by getting Detective Clarke away from his captors before getting the international criminal and heading to the aircraft. Executing the plan, Mack knocked out and bound the guards, replacing Detective Clarke's place in the holding cell with the guards. From there, Mack led Detective Clarke at gun point to Sonya Ramekin's quarters. To no surprise, Sonya was sleeping so Mack knocked her out and "fireman carried" her to the awaiting helicopter, avoiding all the patrols with relative ease.

Placing Sonya into the helicopter's restraints, Mack got into the pilot's seat in the cockpit while Tyler climbed into the co-pilot's seat. Without waiting for Detective Clarke to ask whether or not she even knew how to fly the aircraft, Mack started the propellers and lifted off from the Sahara Desert floor. Upon hearing the helicopter, Sonya's men came out to retaliate, but the helicopter could not be seen due to the lack of lights. It was only once she was sure that they were far enough away that Mack put on the lights and broke radio silence.

Detective Murphy contacted the IIA in order to find out where they were going to meet up with them. Mack ended up taking them to an IIA designated camp and landing there, out of sight. They hid the aircraft so that it was secure before they ended up walking to the IIA camp. Their troubles, however, were far from being over because, shortly after their arrival at the camp, a person was found to be murdered.

Before they could go anywhere, they had to solve the case and, considering the fact that the time of death was before Detective Clarke's and Detective Murphy's arrival, they were assigned to the task of solving the mystery. What complicated matters further was the fact that there was a murderer in their midst who just might murder again if the opportunity arose.

Partnered up with Detective Clarke once again, Mackenzie looked into the cause of death . . . that just so happened to be a knife to the heart. What that led the detective to deduce was that the murderer was familiar with the victim because it had been a frontal attack. It was because of all this inferred information; Mack thought that the murderer was a friend or a lover. Mack gathered everyone together, but, in order to follow her hunch, she kept everyone waiting as she executed the equipment check on every bag and article of clothing as everyone looked on.

Finally, a couple of people couldn't handle it, proclaiming their guilt in their native language. Maria Grazias and Omar Gonzalez spoke fluent Spanish of what had happened that had resulted in someone's demise.

Apparently, what had happened was a lover's quarrel of sorts because, the victim, Arturo Garcia, had thought that Omar was stealing Maria from him. The end result was the confrontation that escalated to murder as Omar plunged the blade into Arturo's chest in plain view of Maria. It was clear that Omar did the killing. However, Maria's role in the entire ordeal suggested that she was an accessory to murder due to the fact that she didn't come forth as a witness or report the incident. It was because of this that the two were arrested and the two detectives could return to the United States of America, but there was still one other person with a different idea in mind.

It seemed as though, they would never get back home and that Mack wouldn't be able to receive the necessary R&R (rest and relaxation) that would keep her performing at her peak detective prowess with the complete ability to analyze and deduce with mysterious mystery-solving rationalization. Thankfully, based on a hunch of hers, Mack checked all the vehicles and modes of transportation, which led Mack to realize the meticulous work of a saboteur in their midst.

Now, Mack had dealt with saboteurs in the past. However, in this particular instance, this saboteur was rather clever. In fact, if Mack had any cause or reason to be a saboteur, she would have done something similar or the exact same thing as this saboteur had done. There was only one problem with how this particular deed had been done and that was the fact which showed that the sabotage was meant to disable the vehicles and other modes of transport at a later time.

By Mack's calculations, done by a simple algorithm in her head, the saboteur wanted them to be ambushed, at a certain time and location. Based upon those calculations, Mack figured out the estimated time of ambush. Quietly rectifying the saboteur's work, Mack could only take the necessary precaution when dealing with such a person that was available to her. The rest of her plan of action resided on a certain amount of luck and just plain Mackenzie Murphy Madness.

Due to the fact that she was the one who "requisitioned" the unauthorized, non-IIA helicopter, Mack was able to fly the aircraft once again. Since the helicopter had been hidden in a strategic location away from the actual IIA camp, it wasn't figured into the saboteur's plan of ambush which made it a wild card, so to speak.

Reading the faces of each IIA personnel present, Mack figured out who the saboteur was before they even loaded up. When they were about ready to leave, Mack spoke briefly with Detective Clarke saying, "Be sure to watch out for Günter Kuhn. You'll know when to watch out for him because it will be when everything gets crazy, even crazier than usual."

"Mack, I'm not sure what you're talking about, but I'll be sure to keep an eye out for Günter since that's what you want."

"It is, but you'd better make it two eyes instead of one since you need both eyes on him once that all goes down. If you need me, I'll be in the sky with that helicopter from Sonya's encampment as my wings."

"Okay, sounds good, Mack. Good luck." Mackenzie Murphy acknowledged him with a nod as she went out of sight to where the helicopter was. Waiting for everyone to leave, she double checked her map in the cockpit in order to figure out where the location would be based on the estimated time of ambush that she had previously figured out. Detective Murphy had time to spare as she jotted down a quick poem about the madness that lurked within.

The poem, that she dubbed Madness's Moment, was a poem that went like this:

> Fear is at the heart of all failure
> So have courage and be sure.
> Madness is of the moment and memory
> So don't be afraid to tell of insanity's story.
> Face today's fears and sorrows,
> Madness might consume all tomorrows.

If Mack had had any doubts of intentionally going into an ambush, that quick poem and her thoughts quelled any thoughts to the contrary of crazy. Mack had made sure that Detective Clarke was in the first vehicle in the convoy with an earpiece radio and both the troublemakers: Günter Kuhn and Sonya Ramekin were safely nestled into their seats. Taking off, the helicopter propelled into the sky, Mack's aircraft lifted up with the pilot not afraid to die even if it was on ground or in the sky.

Approaching fifteen minutes after takeoff, Mack noticed dust to their right and left of the convoy which was a sure sign of what was to come as Mackenzie Murphy told Detective, well, Agent Tyler Clarke, to have the convoy stop. It was at this notification, down at the convoy, that Günter gave the message to move in.

Unaware of the helicopter in the sky, before the ambush could be made, Mack's helicopter swooped in and fired off some bullets, letting a couple of rockets be launched from the aircraft. This dissuaded the ambushers while, in the convoy, Günter was furious, especially when Tyler arrested him. After Günter had been firmly restrained, Agent Clarke gave the order to proceed. With Mack watching their backs, they had no further problems as they made it to the airport.

Once there, the IIA took in all the guilty culprits and, with a brief farewell, they left Mack standing there, feeling a sense of accomplishment. However, at the same time, she felt a sense of loss that threatened to overwhelm her. Shaking those feelings off, Mack hoisted what stuff she had with her, which wasn't much, and boarded the airplane that would take her home.

Exhausted from a certain amount of sleep deprivation, Mack fell asleep even before the airplane was even taxiing to take off. Dreaming, a spectacular river rushed by as she fished off of its rocky shoreline. Nearby, a wet dog lay sprawled out in the sun after some water recreation. With a tent and an internal frame pack, it looked like a scene from an adventure magazine, but it looked, felt, and was real by all appearances because . . . it was all the madness of Mackenzie Murphy.

CASE 27 ACTIVITIES:
CRITICAL THINKING:

This case mentions the fact that Detective Clarke is sent to the Sahara Desert and Detective Murphy ends up coming to the desert as well. Where is the Sahara Desert located? What are some additional facts about the Sahara and deserts in general? Research the Sahara desert and deserts, writing a paragraph or two on your findings.

REVIEW QUESTIONS:

1) Who contacts Detective Murphy regarding a prospective new case for her? Why do they contact her specifically?

2) What event led to Detective Clarke's capture? How could this have been avoided?

3) What measures did Sonya enforce to prevent Detective Murphy or anyone else from entering into the camp? Why were these measures ineffective?

4) How did the skills that Detective Murphy had help when escaping from the criminal's camp and heading to the IIA's campsite?

VOCABULARY REVIEW:

Unscramble the word and write down the word's definition.

duuaosr- strenuous, tiring _____

VOCABULARY:
Define and use in a sentence based on the definition for the word.

Adversaries-

_____

Retaliate-

_____

Inferred-

_____

Algorithm-

_____

Plausible-

_____

Deniability-

_____

Meticulous-

_____

Sabotuer-

_____

CASE 28:
CASE OF THE CONCERT CONFUSION

A Detective Mackenzie Murphy and friend had been planning to go to a concert since they had first heard about it. However, they didn't expect to volunteer until the opportunity presented itself. That's when the spontaneity of Mack's friend came to the surface and they ended up volunteering. Her friend, Savannah Engle had convinced Mack to come to this concert, partly to tear her mind off of Detective Tyler Clarke, her previous partner who was still working for the IIA and partly because of a bet. However, the idea was a good one, but it would have been better if they had just rented a movie.

They were assigned to a vendor booth on the bottom floor, nearby a main door, which could only complicate things. The thrill of meeting a band member before the mass moved in was quite enthralling for Savannah. However, for Detective Murphy, it was admittedly: nerve-wracking. There was no end to the possibility of dangerous scenarios playing through her logical rational mind; the same mind that raged within the maniacal madness of Mackenzie Murphy. It was very fortunate when the initial rush settled down so that Mack was finally able to quell her over-active imagination regarding deadly scenarios.

While the selling and buying of the consumerism with both the consumer and vendor present, it was safe to say that Savannah and Mack settled into a bit of a routine.

That was a routine that was easily adaptable and, as it turned out, easily disrupted.

Somewhere and sometime between the start of the concert and in the time of the event, there was a catastrophe that had taken place, unknown to the people all around the concert. It was as a security guard was going by that he caught Detective Murphy's eyes and halted in his tracks, coming over to her booth. He indicated for her to follow, leaving Mack to follow him out of the public's view. Taking a deep breath to calmly speak his message, he said, "I recognized you as the famous Alaskan detective, Mackenzie Murphy and I would like to ask for your help. We have a corpse and we really need a detective's help right about now."

"I'll help. Get the security footage of that area from the time that people were allowed in until now: including when security and the set-up crews arrived. I'll also need to be shown the corpse to get an estimated time of death and see what we're dealing with: whether it is suicide, homicide or some sort of freak accident. Is that clear or do I have to repeat myself?"

The security guard shook his head and said, "I've got that, Detective. We'll start working on this matter right away. Come with me to the corpse and I'll radio for the security footage as well as get some help for your friend at the booth."

Mack nodded and said, "Sounds good." She was then led to the crime scene. Being in the mindset of a detective, she took note of the injuries, consistent with a fall from the third story. That eliminated quite a few people because only security personnel and a few other "selected" people could go up there. That fact and the injuries ruled out a suicide or a freak accident, leaving only homicide as an option.

The question was: who was the murderer and how could the investigators go about finding that person without causing widespread pandemonium? That led Mack to review the security footage around the time of death to find out who the murderer was and had the evidence to support an arrest. Thankfully for Detective Mackenzie Murphy, there was a judge present at the concert who was willing to give her a couple of arrest warrants to get the issue resolved and to put the culprit away behind bars. The next issue was arresting the culprit once they were able to do so.

However, any celebration was short-lived because the person managed to get loose on the second floor and Detective Murphy was sent sprawling down to her sure death. The culprit was taken down to the ground by the security that was present. The person was then turned over to the local authorities that had finally showed up once the culprit was under control. It was then that a security guard was able to check for a pulse on Detective Murphy who had landed on the corpse of the previous victim, Drew Handwritty. Thankfully, there was a pulse and they instantly called for an ambulance to take the detective to the emergency room. An ambulance arrived within minutes, allowing a prompt removal of the detective who seemed in critical condition. After all that, the security guard, who was the first person to ask for Detective Murphy's help, came up to her friend somewhat reluctantly.

Taking her aside, the security guard informed Savannah of the situation and the fact that her friend was now in the hospital. Overhearing all of this was a band member of the booth they had been running. Savannah, a little distraught, thanked the security guard before she returned to the booth to finish up the last 45 minutes of the concert.

When the concert was over, the reality sunk in some more and the entire band approached her. The person who had overheard the security guard's conversation with her spoke up, saying, "Hi, I couldn't help but overhear that your friend, the other volunteer, is in the hospital and we just wanted to express our gratitude. We hope that your friend pulls through all right."

"Thank you. I really appreciate it and I'm sure that Mackenzie will."

"Is your friend Mackenzie Murphy? The detective?"

"She is, but why do you ask?"

"It just so happens that you're talking with some fans of hers."

"You're joking right? You've been able to meet her practically all night and you just happen to be fans of hers?"

"Yes, that's right. Do you know which hospital she is in?"

"Yes, she's at a hospital here in Boise that I have an address for. They were taking her to the emergency room there."

"Could you do us a favor then? Give her this from us then and tell her to give us a call anytime."

"Okay," Savannah said, taking the card that they provided, kind of shocked at the way things had turned out. After driving from the concert to the hospital, it was then that she found out that Mack was in a coma. The doctors and medical staff didn't know if she would make it or not. That is when Savannah decided to call Detective Matthew Murphy and inform him of the situation and in return, Matthew informed Detective Tyler Clarke.

Both of them were currently working on a case for the IIA where the victim was an international diplomat found dead on US soil. Unable to do anything but solve the case, they went after the mercenaries who had been behind the homicide and after one mercenary in particular, Jack Andrews. Their case led them to California where they ended up in a big confrontation of the mercenaries; however, they were able to get their man.

In the process, Detective Clarke had received a gunshot wound to his arm and suffered minor cuts and abrasions from some shattered glass. Detective Matthew Murphy, on the other hand, didn't have a scratch on him despite his role in the mercenaries' capture. They ended up leaving the mercenaries in the IIA's custody solving the case before they drove towards Boise Idaho where Detective Mackenzie Murphy was.

If the two detectives had thought that their day of action was over, it wasn't. On the way to their destination, they witnessed an accident so they had to pull over. While the emergency services were coming, they had to make sure that the people involved were all right. Afterwards, they had to give their statements that only prevented them further from being at their fellow detective's side, not to mention the friend or family member part of that description of Mack.

Thankfully for them, an officer heard of their problems and escorted them to the border of Oregon and California, wishing them good luck before they departed company. Then, after all that, they ended up in road construction for quite a while. However, they finally made it into Boise after Mack had been in the hospital and in a coma for almost two days. No one knew whether she would live or not.

One of Mackenzie's friends had left a CD for Mackenzie in the event that she came out of her coma, but most spent some time talking to her. Some, like Detective Tyler Clarke talked to her until he fell asleep, dreaming of many cases and instances where Mackenzie's smile and unique humor had caught him off guard.

On that note, Tyler dreamed of Mackenzie's father, Matthew, escorting her down the aisle, only for her to choose a sled dog out from a dog enclosure. She then left, down the aisle, out the door, and into the blinding snow that awaited her. Detective Clarke had tried to chase after her as he heard music from somewhere, but couldn't reach her. She ended up fading into the whiteness, lost from his sight. The dream faded into nothingness as he succumbed to the darkness of deep sleep. That brought the conclusion of the case of the Concert Confusion of the Detective Mackenzie Murphy Series. Be sure to check out the next case to find out what happened to Detective Mackenzie Murphy of whether or not she comes out of her coma or is left in a state of coma chaos.

To Be Continued....

CASE 28 ACTIVITIES

CRITICAL THINKING:

Concerts are a form of entertainment that people often enjoy going to. What different bands perform in your region? Have you ever been to a concert? What would it be like to go to one? What was your favorite concert? Write a paragraph or two regarding concerts.

REVIEW QUESTIONS:

1) How did the person's recognition of Detective Murphy result in her involvement with the case at the concert? Who was it that had recognized her and why?

2) In your opinion, would Detective Murphy have been glad to be given the case to get away from the booth at the concert? Why or why not?

3) With all the people in the concert building, how could such a catastrophe happen without someone seeing something suspicious? Would someone have mentioned something if they had or just ignored it and continued on watching the concert?

4) What would the friend of the detective, Savannah, be thinking initially when informed of what was going on? What would your reaction be in that same situation?

5) What was the reason that Detective Clarke and Detective Matthew Murphy were not present when Mack was initially hurt, even though Matthew Murphy lives near the area where Mack was visiting?

VOCABULARY:

Define and use in a sentence based on the definition for the word.

Catastrophe-

_____

_____

VOCABULARY REVIEW:

Unscramble the word and write down the word's definition.

Uoiiacmls – evil, intentioned

_____

rsuepoil- hazardous

_____

treeeddt-disuaded , discouraged.

_____

CASE 29:
COMA CHAOS

Detective Mackenzie Murphy was dressed in all white as it sparkled in the light. She was escorted down the aisle of the church with friends and family all around. With her father's arm in hers, they made it to the altar where Detective Tyler Clarke waited for her. Once there, at the altar with flowers all around, her father, Matthew Murphy, ran out of the room, followed by Tyler Clarke, leaving Mackenzie there at the altar all alone. She ended up walking out of the room and changing, perplexed at what had just happened. Putting on a bullet-proof vest, she vacated the room when a person with a gun took her hostage. What in the world was happening-was a question that came to mind when she was taken into a plain white room. She was further perplexed by their questions: "Did you know that your father is an agent for the CIA?"

"No."

"What about your fiancé? Did he know?"

"I'm not sure."

"You're not sure, why not?"

"It's because I've just barely gotten here. I only remember walking down the aisle and nothing before that."

"Our records here show otherwise and, Ms. Murphy, with your reputation as a detective how could you not know about your father's profession as a CIA agent? Either you are covering up for him or that blow to your head has taken a far greater toll than what you've let on."

"I assure you, Sir, although it may appear that I've lost my mind, I haven't lost my memory yet. The basis regarding this matter is because, the last recollection I have, I was at a concert and not even engaged yet, so what is this all about? I don't even think that this is happening or real for that matter." Mack said before she stopped, looking rather determined and defiant of the situation that she was now in.

Annoyed and under a time restraint, the person in charge said, "This is getting us nowhere, let's leave her here and maybe she will think twice about being so difficult."

They left Detective Mackenzie there in that room, making a couple of mistakes in the process. The first one was that they had left her in cuffs without checking whether or not she had a key, which Mack, of course, had in her possession. Then the second mistake was the fact that they left her unsupervised with not even a video surveillance to keep an eye on her. That left her to her own Murphy Madness that was all too famous. All she really had to do was to recover the cuff key from its hidden location and to unlock the cuffs on herself. Now, that was the easy part of the escape and the next part, for an experienced person like Mackenzie, was slightly harder than a walk in the park, but definitely easier than a full-fledged marathon.

Either way, she came out of the room and disguised herself as a janitor with a spare set of janitor keys that she'd acquired. No one even really noticed her, busy at their own duties and tasks. She managed to get out of there before she had another problem to remedy: she didn't know where she was. When she finally figured out where she was, Mackenzie wished that she had never found out because she was in: . . . Texas. She had never ever wanted to go to Texas and she was none too happy about it either. It was like finding out that someone had a horrible disease, especially if that someone was you.

Regardless, Mackenzie went to a pay phone and called up her friend, one of her many friends and they agreed to buy her airplane ticket to Idaho. All she had to do was to make it to the Dallas airport.

For a detective, that was the easy part, but, for a detective wanted for questioning, it was slightly harder to get on board an airplane than usual. To remedy that problem, Mackenzie visited a thrift store and bought a disguise that consisted of a shawl, a cane, hair dye, and several articles that would make for a convincing masquerade. She then changed into her disguise before making her way to the airport. When she got her ticket, the person who gave it to Mack had to do a double take before she said, "Here you go Ms. Murphy."

Mack responded in a raspy, old, thin voice saying, "Thank you, Dearie." She was successful in her disguise and she made it to Idaho just fine. From there, it was to be a battle of wits, a chessboard puzzle, so to speak, to find out what was happening to her and why her father was now a CIA agent. Of course, right in the middle of this madness, it would be Mackenzie Murphy who would stumble onto a murder mystery.

This one in particular was one of the hardest that she had ever stumbled across. There wasn't the tiniest shred of evidence, even for her logical rationalizing mind. Sure, there was a corpse, shredded beyond recognition, but there was no DNA, fingerprints, residue, murder weapon or anything to go with other than conjecture and theory other than the victims' identity. It brought her literally to the brink of madness and aggravated her with a surprising amount of frustration.

On top of it all, she was fatigued and in need of some rest & relaxation (R&R). Also, the thought of finding out about her father never really lost its luster because it seemed that reality clashed with reality. She just didn't know what was dream and what reality was any more. The added confusion of her mental problems only made the case that much more complicated. It had already been given up on as a cold case even though it had just taken place in the last 24 hours and that is how Mackenzie got it: as a new cold case.

Like all humans, Detective Murphy was bound to make a mistake sometime and although she recognized that there must be a connection with a government agency, she wasn't prepared to be assaulted by ten CIA agents. All of this was just to get her into their vehicles, closely followed by the people who had questioned her earlier. Once inside the black SUV, her father sat before her to say, "Hi there Mackenzie. Sorry to drag you into this, but you mustn't solve that case. Some mysteries are best left unsolved like the reason you're here. Just leave it all alone."

"Is this coming from my father, because the Matthew Murphy I know would jump at the chance to solve a mystery and wouldn't be a CIA agent. So tell me this: what's going on here, Dad?"

His daughter's statement caught him off guard for just a moment before Matthew Murphy spoke again, in a soft voice, "Mackenzie, I know what you must be going through, but you have to trust me on this matter: don't solve that case. It's just not worth it because it won't solve anything. Is that clear?"

"Yes, that's clear."

"And another thing, stay away from Tyler Luke Clarke."

"Why?"

"No good can come from him, no matter what your relationship is with him."

"Okay," Mackenzie replied and she was dropped off shortly afterwards. Now, under normal circumstances, Mackenzie wouldn't have dreamed of ever disobeying her father, but with him as a CIA agent, these weren't normal circumstances.

The first rebellious act that she did was to set out to solve the case. Aggravated and spurned to action by being told what not to do, she grit her teeth and got to work solving the mystery, which led her to the CIA. There had been a cover-up and Mack gave the suspect's identity and the evidence to local law enforcement.

As they went to arrest the suspect, Mackenzie laid low, keeping a low profile and subtly contacting Tyler Luke Clarke, supposedly her fiancé. He was going to meet her in a crowded movie theater and Mackenzie realized that something was different right away. Watching from a distance, she had the chance to observe that he wasn't alone and that he was being followed. About 20 minutes into the movie, Mack pulled the fire alarm, causing everyone to rush out in a panic, giving her the opportunity to pull Tyler into the janitorial closet. "Tell me what's going on?"

Tyler looked at her and said, "Mack, there is something that you should know. First, I love you and I'm sorry that I left you at the altar. The second is that when you saved the president's life, the person was actually after you, but he unintentionally made you a hero. He's going to come after you again and when he does, it won't be pretty. You have enemies Mackenzie, more enemies than you or I know."

"Why are you with others and why are you being followed?"

"I've been working with the IIA and I was helping them catch a well-known criminal with the mafia. The mafia got wind of it and they've been following me, calling for extra security in all my dealings, personal and professional. Does that help?"

"Yes, one last thing before we go our separate ways." Mackenzie kissed him, placing something in his hand before she made her way to her friend's vehicle in the parking lot.

Mackenzie drove to where she was staying, noting whether or not she had been followed. Once there, it was about eleven o'clock so she went to sleep, dreaming strange dreams in her restless sleep. In her dreams, she was in a hospital and people kept coming and going with no rhyme or reason. She saw sad solemn faces, leaving her to wonder: am I in a coma? If so, how do I get out of here? When she woke, it was with a start and she realized what she needed to do. Mack quickly got dressed and took some coffee in a to-go mug while a plan was quickly being formed in her mind, solidified with every passing minute.

She left a note for her friend, borrowing one of their vehicles and heading to downtown Boise. As she went along, Mack realized that she was being followed. Unable to see their faces in the tinted window of the threatening appearing vehicle, she realized that it was the mafia, as unheard of as it was. She decided to confront them, which might not have been the smartest idea, but for an aggravated, annoyed detective, it seemed like the right thing to do at the time. Putting on her caution lights, she pulled off to the edge of the road, only to have the mafia vehicle behind her do the same. Five men in tuxedos stepped out, each with a pistol or weapon in hand. The person, obviously in charge, stepped up to her window and said, "Our boss would like to talk with you. It's about going home."

"What if I don't want to go home?"

"Then we'll have to bring you in. You can't stay here forever, Detective Mackenzie Murphy and either way, you're coming."

Mack showed them her weapons and said, with a steely determination, "Leave me alone." Thankfully for both sides, they backed off and left Mackenzie to go to the hospital. Once there, she felt in a dream-like state, letting herself go to where her feet led her.

She ended up in an empty room where she was told by someone, "It's not time yet. The greatest mystery of all hasn't been solved yet."

"But I've already solved the case, it's closed. Why keep me here?"

"Can I help you?" a concerned nurse asked her.

"No, sorry, I must have just come to the wrong room."

The nurse was still rather concerned and said, "Here, at least let me have a look at you. I'm on my break, but you need it more than I do."

"Thanks," Detective Murphy replied before the nurse checked her out and said, "It seems as though you've had some sort of trauma. I would like to have you take it easy. If put in the wrong situation, you could very well have issues and any number of problems could happen."

"Okay, thank you." Detective Mackenzie Murphy left, going out the hospital's entrance, hoping to do just that, take it easy...until the mafia showed up and took her to California, blindfolded so that she wouldn't be able to tell where she was. However, no one ever thought to check her watch that seemed ordinary enough, but it was hardly ordinary. When a certain button was pressed, it would light up and show the location.

When meeting "the boss", she had a particular advantage, but that was nothing compared to what the circumstances presented her with. "The Boss" turned out to be Tyler Luke Clarke, the head of the mafia, so now Mackenzie not only had a CIA agent for a father, but now she had a mafia boss as a lover.

"Mack," Tyler said, breaking her musings, "do you now know why your father was so keen as to disapprove of me? Are things making more sense?"

"Tyler, things haven't been making sense for a while now. Honestly, I just don't know anymore." Tyler, seeing that his men were wary of him being soft, sent them off with a wave of his gun hand, signifying to them to leave them alone. Setting the gun on the table, he came over to her and kissed her.

When she opened her eyes from the kiss, Mack was no longer in California with the mafia, but in the hospital. Her father and Detective Tyler Clarke were there to greet her and she realized what the person had meant about 'the greatest mystery of all hasn't been solved yet'. It was the mystery of love and Mack had found it because she loved and was loved.

That was the ultimate mystery and that was what brought her back, because it was a mystery that she hadn't solved. Seeing her father and previous partner together reminded her of the situation she just had. Waking up in the hospital, it was all that she could notice was how strange the actual reality was after experiencing what could only be considered a different way of thinking.

Soon after coming back to reality, she was exhausted, falling asleep and dreaming of dog sledding. In her dream, she was no longer running on snow, but training with an all-terrain vehicle or four-wheeler as it was known across the Alaskan terrain. Everything seemed as though it was based on an actual memory of her training days. It was a memory when she worked as a dog handler for one winter that secured not only her willingness to teach, but also her passion for dogs, concluding case #29: Coma Chaos of the Detective Mackenzie Murphy Series.

CASE 29 ACTIVITIES:

CRITICAL THINKING:

In this case, Detective Murphy is in a coma where she is experiencing a dream about an alternate reality. What would it be like to be under the impression that things were different? How would you feel in a situation like this? What would you do or what could you do? If you were in Detective Murphy's position, what would you have done differently or the same? Write down a paragraph regarding what an instance like what Mack underwent would be like if you were in her shoes.

REVIEW QUESTIONS:

1) What complicated the wedding? What would you have been thinking if you were one of the guests? What do you think Mack was thinking?

2) In this case, Detective Murphy is not particularly happy after she is lost in an unknown location. Where does that location turn out to be? Why is the return trip complicated?

3) Why does Detective Matthew Murphy discourage Mack from solving a case? What was her reaction to this discouragement?

4) Why does Detective Mack Murphy go against her father's wishes regarding Tyler Clarke? What is the result?

5) How does a realization help bring Mack out of a coma? In your opinion, what might be the reciprocating result in the actual reality be from this case?

VOCABULARY:
Define and use in a sentence based on the definition for the word.

Perplexed-_____

Defiant-_____

Masquerade-_____

Conjecture-_____

Luster-_____

VOCABULARY REVIEW:

Unscramble the word and write down the word's definition.

eelmmpudt- plunged; fell

_____

CASE 30:
ALTAR ABANDON

A month had passed since the case of the concert confusion and Mackenzie's own experience with coma chaos. It had been because of the latter that she was now in her current position: dressed and veiled in a gown of white. What did that have to do with the coma chaos case? Love, because Mackenzie had come to recognize her love for Detective Tyler Clarke.

Now, here she was, preparing to be married with white roses all around. The day was turning into a beautiful day for Mackenzie to be married. She approached the altar on her father's arm and met up with Tyler there, being reassured by the smile on his face. They said their vows and "I dos" before the preacher asked if there was any objections and both of their hearts sank when there was an objection. It was an objection from the President of the United States of America that had the entire crowd of friends and family silent.

Pulling Detective Clarke and Mack aside, he said, "There's been a situation. I regret to inform you that you'll have to postpone your wedding and honeymoon because I need my best detectives on this."

"Do we have any choice in the matter?"

"No. So come on, we have your transportation waiting for you and you can change on the flight."

"Okay."

Detectives Mackenzie Murphy and Tyler Clarke took one moment to say to everyone there as they were coming back through: "Feel free to have some food." They ran down the aisle, hand-in-hand, and out the door without another word, leaving all the people in attendance shocked by the turn of events.

They were escorted to a black limousine and taken to the airport where they had a private, presidential jet waiting to take them to their next destination. They changed on board the aircraft before they met with the president, who briefed them on the pressing case that was facing them. He said, "Detectives, the case in the folder before you is confidential first and foremost. Secondly, it needed to be solved yesterday if you get what I mean."

"Yes. What exactly are we supposed to do about this case? We've usually solved murder mysteries and this is more of a missing person case."

"Detective Mackenzie Lynn Murphy, you are an intelligent person. What do you think the answer is to that?"

"I think the answer, Mr. President, is that it is a detective's duty to deduce and, regardless of the case, that analytical deduction must be put to work. This case is rather practical and though we haven't solved too many missing person type of cases, I believe that this is rather solvable."

"All right. That certainly answers that question. Now what do you need to solve this case?"

"First: coffee. After that, we're going to need a list of relations, friends, acquaintances, and anyone who might have come in contact with the victim. Along with that, there needs to be a list of anyone who might have come in contact with the victim's relations. The victim might be just a pawn in a larger chess board. Then we will need any information about the person in question. In other words, a suspect list of essentially everyone that could be a possibility. Transportation would be nice along with access to a lab with technology would be recommended."

"That will be done. Is there anything else?"

"There's just one thing. If we solve this . . . I mean when we solve this, will we actually be able to resume our personal lives or will you just send us on another case?"

"I'll let you resume your personal lives and organize the wedding for both of you. That is after you solve this case, of course."

"Of course, I wouldn't expect anything less. That sounds great." Of course, at the time, Mackenzie had no way of knowing just what lay in store for them regarding the case. By just glancing at the case, Mack knew that there was more to it than met the eye and that there must be a ransom involved somewhere. It had all the characteristics of a ransom and black mail: a wealthy, politically-involved family with a semi-rebellious teenager. After a few moments, Mackenzie asked, "So what's the ransom?"

"What do you mean?"

"This case is typical of a hostage-ransom situation so what's the ransom?"

"They want 1.5 million."

"When and where is the exchange supposed to take place?"

"Today at five o'clock with no weapons by those who bring the money."

"Great, I'll be there and give them the money."

"The clients don't have the money for them. That's part of the problem."

Mack looked at him for a second before saying, "That's no problem: I do. All I have to do is finding where the person is after the ransom is given and ensure that I keep my money."

"Okay, that sounds like a plan. I can tell that you want to get this case solved before it's too late."

"Yes sir. Mr. President, I want to get this solved." Mackenzie replied as she made a couple more inquiries to find out the location of the ransom before she made a couple more phone calls to be assured that the ransom money would be available.

When the time came, Mack had the money and went to the place weaponless, only armed with her wits. Hand cuffed to the case, she was prepared for any problem that could complicate things . . . every problem that is, except waking up to see a very concerned Detective Tyler Clarke.

"Mack, are you all right? You just fell and hit your head." Tyler said, making Mackenzie Murphy take in the details and realize that she had a concussion that had made her pass out. After the coma chaos case, as it was dubbed by someone, Mack had never wanted that type of experience to happen to her ever again, but it just did.

As reality sunk in, Mackenzie realized that she was on ice: the ice of the river where the Yukon Quest would finish in a couple of hours. Finally able to have a firm grasp on reality, she said, looking into Detective Tyler Clarke's eyes, "I have a head ache and a concussion, but nothing that I haven't had before."

"Good," Tyler said with a bit of smile: "Because we need your help, or rather: he does." He said as he was indicating towards the President of the United States.

"What's going on?" Mack asked, genuinely intrigued.

"There's been a murder, or at least an attempted murder and you have to solve it in an hour."

"Why is it only an hour?"

"Because, that's how long we have until the nitroglycerine or bomb goes off."

"Great, is there anything else?"

"No, there is nothing else at the moment. Other than this packet of detailed information and list of possible suspects, I have nothing else for you other than to wish you good luck." Mack took the packet from Detective Tyler Clarke, but it wasn't until she was safely within the confines of a building that she opened and analyzed the case.

Despite its intricacy, Mackenzie felt like someone tackling a puzzle, thrilled with the challenge of putting the pieces together. Still, there was something wrong with this entire scenario and it was until the last few minutes that she realized where the bomb was and who the culprit was. The only problem was that Mack realized that there were multiple bombs and that each of the suspects was responsible. There was only one innocent suspect in the list of five people that she was provided. With ten seconds remaining, as the winner was coming into the finish, Detective Mack Murphy was radioed the all clear, making it another successful case before she woke up for real this time. . .in her bed back at home-her home-in Fairbanks

Alaska. That's when her phone rang and she picked it up, saying, "Hello?"

"Is this Detective Mackenzie Murphy?"

"Yes, it is. What's this about?"

"This is about your father, Detective Matthew Murphy; he's in a hospital in Idaho. I'd recommend that you come see him. This is the chief of police of Nampa, Phil Putnam, for your information."

"Thank you, Chief. Do you know what hospital?"

"Yes, the Nampa Medical Center. Do you want the address?"

"Yes," Mack, with pen and paper in hand wrote down the address that they provided before saying, "Thank you. Bye." Mack got off the phone without waiting for a response of "good-bye" from the chief before grabbing her bags, coffee, and heading for the door. Thankfully Mackenzie knew of several pilots and was able to get a flight to Boise within minutes of being in cell service.

Once in Boise, she got a ride to Nampa and to the Medical Center, where it became apparent - this wasn't going to be a stress-free trip. She also realized that the dreams she had were based on actual memories from when she was younger. Now, as she stood before her father's bedside, it took her back to other times. She was startled out of her thoughts when her father said, "Mack, I didn't expect to see you here."

"Well, I didn't expect to see you here either. What happened this time?"

"Murphy's Law: what can go wrong, will. I was working on a case and things went from bad to worse. Kind of like your wedding and the case that disrupted it all." Mack realized at that moment that the case with the president actually happened, but why couldn't she remember the details of what had happened? As he continued listening, Mack learned about the particular of the case in the soothing words of her father, "The President was very sorry that you were held hostage and that Detective Clarke was caught in the crossfire. You, of course, had the situation under control so there was no need for him to order in Detective Clarke to rescue you. Since then and the incident at the Yukon Quest finish, things haven't been the same between the two of you, especially with your memory loss."

It was then that it all came back to her and Mack wiped away some tears in her eyes. "Thanks dad. I remember now, I thought that it was just a dream . . . but it was real. I'll have to talk with Tyler about all of it. I hope that you'll be all right, but as you always use to tell me: 'Hey, we're Murphy's - tough as nails, right!'"

Mack hugged her father gently before she left the hospital and made a phone call. After two rings, it was answered with a "Hello?"

"Tyler?"

"Yes?"

"This is Mack."

"Is everything okay?"

"Yes, I just remembered today about the wedding wronged and the Yukon Quest. I'm sorry about it all."

"It's okay. Mackenzie, where are you?"

"In Idaho visiting my dad, why?"

"It's 4:47 a.m. right now. I didn't think that you would be in Alaska calling me at this time."

"Oh, I'm so sorry. I'll call you when I'm back in Fairbanks."

"Okay. Bye Mack." They hung up and Mack Murphy phoned the pilot again to secure another flight to Alaska.

Once the plane landed, she had a ride ready and waiting for her. Detective Clarke, wearing aviator sun glasses, was there to greet her. Without waiting to grab her luggage, Mack approached Detective Tyler Clarke and hugged him. Tears coming to her eyes, she said, "Tyler, I'm so sorry. How do you even put up with my insanity?"

"Because, Mack, it was your insanity that made me sane and gave me a name. I'm no longer the officer I was when I first met you. Kenzie, you've made me into the detective I am."

"It's because of you that I'm no longer who I was either. I'm no longer an elementary school teacher, although I sometimes teach in a different sense of elementary as a detective. Sometimes, I'm trapped within two different worlds: the one that was and the one that I want to be. No amount of deduction can ever hope to rescue me from my state of entrapment. Can you help me by bringing me back to reality?"

Tyler took off his sunglasses and said, "Yes Mack, I believe I can." Getting on one knee, he said, "Mackenzie Lynn Murphy, will you marry me so that I might make us a world together?"

"Yes, I will. Hopefully this time . . . there will be no objections from anyone." Mack said and quickly embraced him, knowing full well what challenges and happiness lay ahead.

One month later. . .

Dressed in white, once again, Mackenzie Lynn Murphy walked down the aisle with her arm held by her father. In attendance, there were the president and several other friends and family of the couple being betrothed in matrimony. Presented to Tyler Luke Clarke was Mackenzie from the arm of her father, Detective Matthew Murphy.

The entire scene was in Mack's dreams, being swept away in a sweeping scene like the Aurora Borealis on a snowy moonlit night. There was only one phrase that could be said as the stain glass window shed its multi-colored light and that was the words: "I do." Leaving the deducing detective, deduction less, but not dreamless. For this was the beginning of a 'dream come true. . .' concluding Case #30 Altar Abandon of the Detective Mackenzie Lynn Murphy Series.

CASE 30 ACTIVITIES:

CRITICAL THINKING:

This case specifically mentions the Yukon Quest, a dog sled race, which brings about the question: Where does this race take place? Some races have alternate starts or courses. What does the Yukon Quest do in regards to that? How long is the race? Who competes in it? When does it take place? How much is the purse for the finishers? How does that race compare with other dog sled races like the Iditarod? Write a paper regarding the Yukon Quest based on your research.

REVIEW QUESTIONS:

1) What event disrupted the wedding that the two detectives were having? What was the reason behind this disruption?

2) Although it didn't specifically mention the details about the first case, what information leads you to the conclusion that it was solved? What character helps fill in the gaps about the cases?

3) What is the problem that occurs with the second case for the dauntless detective? How does Mack prevail against the problem?

4) Where does Detective Murphy go once she has solved both of the cases? What event prompts her travels?

5) What was a primary significant event that takes place in this case? Why is it important regarding the characters?

VOCABULARY:

Define and use in a sentence based on the definition for the word.

Entrapment-

_____

VOCABULARY REVIEW:

Unscramble the word and write down the word's definition.

uynnnaoomssse- unknown; unnamed

_____

Eeenhibliicmporsn; unintelligible; unfathomable

_____

gluvra-crude, rude

_____

CASE 31:
MYSTERY MOVE

As Mackenzie Lynn Murphy Clarke sat at home, it was still strange to see the ring on her finger. It had been a somewhat relaxing time with no pressing cases for her to solve. However, it was as though something big was going to happen. That is when the phone rang and Mack picked it up from its receiver, saying, "Hello?"

"Morning, this is the chief of police and I need you to come down to the station when you can, if you're not too busy."

"I'll be right there, Chief." Mack hung up the phone, grabbing her keys, coffee mug, and a pack that she always had on hand for instances like these where she was called into action for the police. Getting into her vehicle, she drove to the Fairbanks Police Department.

Once there, she met with the chief of police in his office. "Have a seat, Mack. Or, should I say, Detective Mackenzie Murphy Clarke. I hear congratulations are in order. Do you recall what I said a long time ago? Well, it doesn't matter because this department needs you. That's why you're being promoted to Senior Chief Detective. And, here is your first order of business: we're taking advantage of the respite regarding criminal activity to train up some more detectives. As Senior Chief Detective, we want your experience and help on this matter. I realize that this will give you less time in the field, however, based on your record of near-death experiences, it's probably for the best. What do you think, Mack?" The chief asked sincerely.

"Chief, this is a great honor. Is there anyone more qualified for the position or am I the most qualified?"

"Mack, you should know that other than your father, who is actually supposed to be in retirement, you're the most qualified person. In fact, you're probably overqualified for this position. And . . . you'll have an assistant here to help you."

"Who might that be?"

"Detective Tyler Clarke."

"Really?"

"Yes, next to you and your father, he has the next most experience. Plus, he has experience with you and this department. Now, are you up to this task? I think you are, but the question is: do you accept this position?"

"Yes. I'll accept this; however, I do have a couple of questions. First, do I choose the people I teach or do I get the candidates assigned to me?"

"You'll have people assigned to you, but if you find anyone else suited to the position then you can request that person."

"Okay, when will I start?"

"Right now, unless you have any objections."

"Then let's go." Mack followed the chief as he led her to a room with seven people, excluding her husband, Detective Tyler Clarke. Taking in the scene in an instant, she asked, "Might I make a suggestion? You might want to start off with some of the basics that make a good detective. One of which is: T.A.R., that is an acronym that stands for think, analyze and rationalize. In order to become a good detective, you must utilize this skill. That requires practice and, on that note: who am I?"

One person raised their hand and answered, once acknowledged with this response: "You're Detective Mackenzie Murphy, right?"

"I am to a certain degree. Now, explain to me how you came to that conclusion." Mack said.

"I've seen your picture in a newspaper after you solved a case during the Yukon Quest dog sled race," the person's response was to the exercise.

"So, you used facts to come to the conclusion of who I am. However, it's the small details that make up the big picture. Could I have a volunteer?" A quiet observant person raised their hand to be brought forward before the group. This activity was taking place after the chief left the room to go onto other tasks.

Once the student was up front, Mack said, "You're name is Caroline Whitmansen. You've been working as an officer in the legal department despite the assistance you've given to a couple of my colleagues. You haven't had a vacation lately, driven by your work. I could go on, but some of my deductions are of a more personal nature."

Without flinching, Caroline said, "Detective, your deductions were simple on this matter. You saw my name on my paper, ink stains on my hands put me in the legal department, and you've probably heard of some assistance I've given from your colleagues. You've recently have been married and had your honeymoon some place where the sun was shining. You've recently been doing some writing, probably for some record keeping on cases. And, you're also a musher with just a few dogs now, since you've been away so much."

"Good, that is an excellent example of astute observation and T.A.R. Now, we're going to do a few exercises to help develop this skill or fine tune the skills that you already have. You can go ahead and sit back down Caroline. Thank you." For the next hour, Mack showed her abilities as a teacher and before she let them leave, Mack gave them a task: "A month from today, I want each of you to present me with a case that you believe is unsolvable. I'm giving you each a month so that you won't pick a simple burglary or an easy case at the last minute. It'll help me gauge your abilities and confidence level. That is all, have a great day."

Everyone left the room, leaving Detective Mackenzie Murphy Clarke and Detective Tyler Clarke alone. "Hey Mack, I would like to thank you for taking over. It is clear that you're a great teacher and detective. That's why I wanted this assignment for you. Despite all those cases with Murphy's law, I thought that it was about time that you pass on some of those skills you've used for deduction and stay out of harm's way."

"I agree on this matter, since it's about time that I had a break from perilous pursuits and near-death experiences." They hugged before they switched back into the professionalism that made them detectives and went back to help analyze cases. It was also there that they talked with the chief about the training schedule for their detectives-in-training.

One month later. . .

As she was getting ready for everyone to arrive, Mack noticed a brown envelope with her name on it, sitting on a desk. Having sent Tyler for coffee and donuts, she picked up the envelope curiously, her mental reasoning working overtime. Inside it was this note:

Dear famous detective and teacher,

The case file that this envelop contains is completely confidential, for your eyes only. Proceed with all due discretion. . .

It is only because of the fact that your status is still listed as active with the military that this case was even presented to you. I believe that you should know the reason why your status is still active so I won't go into any detail. However, this case is of utmost importance and silence is an essential key on this matter.

Thanks 78326

Reading the case, Mackenzie realized the intricacy of the matter. However, she also knew that other cases would be presented to her and she wanted to be present for those cases. Mack had often found that when she was faced with a particularly difficult case, it helped to look towards inspiration from other aspects in life. Even in her younger years, taking a walk somewhere had given her a perspective that often helped with the case. On that note, when Tyler came back with the coffee and donuts, Mack wasn't surprised to see a couple of detectives-in-training filter into the room with a folder in each of their hands. The folders were presented to Mackenzie who looked each case over, writing who each folder was from on a sticky note attached to the front of it. She did that for all of the case folders before giving them a task to work on while she reviewed the cases.

The task she gave them was to solve a puzzle by piecing together the facts. Each puzzle piece had a square packet around it with an object, person, place, or idea on it. By placing the objects in a certain order, they would essentially solve the case.

As the detectives-in-training were working on solving their cases, not related towards their actual case folders, Mack realized, once she got the last case file, that the last case pertained to the military's case. The only difference was that the case before her now, showed mistakes that pointed out the criminal. There was only one problem and that was the fact that the criminal was someone that Mack knew and had taught. The person was . . . shots rang out and in that moment, she realized that there was more than one culprit as she was hit by a bullet, only to stare down the barrel of a pistol.

There was a pistol that was at the hands of Devin Lyle who said, "Mackenzie Murphy, the famous detective, and previous teacher at the school on Chilly Lane in Fairbanks. I think that you should remember me." He said this with a sneer on his face.

"Yes, I remember you and I understand your reasons. Although, the question is: why did they send you? Surely you've learned more than they have about proper person behavior."

"How do you know that I'm not working alone?"

"It's because of the other two murders presumably committed by your so-called friends."

"They deserved to die and you also deserve to die."

"Freeze! Drop it!" Caroline said, holding a gun to him on one side while Detective Tyler Clarke was on the other side. This was one of the predicaments that Mack was supposed to avoid by teaching. Still, with his attention diverted, she was able to gain the advantage with a quick upward kick, sending the gun flying out of his hands. That's when people moved in to secure the suspect and the situation. No one was killed by any of the shots although Mack had the bullet hit just above the heart where the bullet-proof vest was that she always wore. It had saved her life again.

In light of the gravity of the situation, Mack still was able to say, "And to think that this was supposed to be considerably less life-threatening than field work."

"Mack, when you're involved, even being in the safest place is life-threatening."

"By the way, what is the safest place possible so I can put in a reservation to test and prove your theory?" Mack asked.

"Detective Mackenzie Clarke, there's a military officer here to see you."

"Okay," she said as the officer, a captain at that, cleared his throat.

"Detective, did you receive the case folder?"

"Yes and thanks to a little help, I have it solved."

"Really? So soon? How'd you do that?"

"Simple really, another case that pertained to the confidential case that you guys presented me with was brought to my attention. By solving that case, which practically solved itself, I was able to solve the case that you presented to me."

"Brilliant! The only problem is the unanswered question as to why your status with the military still active?"

"You tell me."

"Apparently, that is very confidential."

"It is and I'm sorry to inform you that due to the secretive nature of that information, I'm unable to discuss that with you, at this time." Mack handed him the case file with the culprit being pointed out by being right in front with a sticky note exclaiming: This is the culprit!

With a nod, before he left, the military captain handed her another folder saying, "You don't have to solve this case if you don't want to, but this case might be of some interest to you. This is unofficially, of course. Good-bye."

With that, he left, leaving Mack's curiosity aroused. Tyler, actually thinking rationally, said, "Mackenzie, you don't need another case."

"To me another case provides a way of escape: to help someone else. I have enough problems in my life so it helps knowing that I can change things around to help someone else with their problems." Picking up the case, Mack couldn't have known then the change of events and issues that would arise from it.

Since the case was of a medical mix-up and now, the victim in the morgue was mislabeled due to a medic's mistake. For this case, Mack found the best means to an end was by retracing the medic's steps through an interview and by actually going to the scene. In the end, she found out that the medic was set up by another medic in an attempt to have the person fired. What was the motive?

The motive was money, because what else would drive someone to utter and complete madness besides love? Despite this, Mack sensed that there was an underlying issue with the health care's corruption. If one medical personnel could be turned towards devious deeds then who could say whether or not others could be corrupted? That left Mack feeling as though she was fighting a losing battle and getting nowhere. Even if she found one corrupt criminal, there was always one more still out there. At least she was able to lay her head down at night, knowing that she had done a good thing. The work that Mack had done during the day had put some culprits away, sending a message that crime for a criminal wouldn't pay: not now nor any other day.

Speaking of day, Mack dreamed of the daylight that she could delight in. It was the kind of daylight that still had snow for her to mush whatever adventure lay ahead. Then reality hit her in her dream that she no longer had Cream, a dog that she had once loved in her team. The snow rained down as it melts in the warmth of the sun, bringing her dream to an abrupt and unfulfilling end as all the snow disappeared in the whisper of the wind, concluding Case #31, the case of the Mystery Move, of the Detective Mackenzie Murphy Series.

CASE 31 ACTIVITIES:

CRITICAL THINKING:

This case involves teaching and training, both of which are valuable things to have. What would it be like to teach? What challenges would it pose? How could the instruction go better in the classroom? In what ways could the teaching be worse? Put yourself in your teacher's shoes. What would that be like? Write a paragraph or two regarding teaching.

Bonus activity: Try teaching a subject to someone. What are your successes? What are your failures? Write notes on what went well and what could go better next time? Hint: it is best to know the subject pretty well that you are trying to teach.

REVIEW QUESTIONS:

1) What is the honor bestowed by the chief of police for Detective Mackenzie Murphy Clarke? Why do you think the detective was awarded this honor?

2) What is the new task that Mack is given? How does this task work better, worse or the same as the previous ventures?

3) How have the dangerous situations involving the detective started improving compared to the previous cases? Why do you think that is?

VOCABULARY:
Define and use in a sentence based on the definition for the word.

Astute-

_____

_____

Intricacy-

_____

_____

Presumably-

_____

_____

Pertained-

_____

_____

Aroused-

_____

_____

VOCABULARY REVIEW:
Unscramble the word and write down the word's definition.

srrriileeebv-permanent, irreparable

_____

CASE 32:
DOCTOR DECEIT

After several years of teaching other people to be detectives, Detective Mackenzie Clarke was presented with a case that reminded her of the last case she had solved before teaching and life took over.

She and Tyler now had a family and she was expecting again, but this was a case that she couldn't refuse, especially since she was able to investigate it as a patient from the inside of the hospital. However, she could hardly have anticipated the effects that would occur as a result of this investigatory case. At least, she was able to do some surveillance instead of the usual stunt of going in blind with both barrels.

In the several years of teaching, Mack had learned to use some more technology for investigatory purposes rather than the old fashioned, trouble-ridden approach. The times were changing and the investigatory means were changing also.

Now Mack had adjusted to the times and came to terms with the passing time of the type of style that she had previously used. Murder mysteries weren't the only cases that a detective would or could solve, although, that seemed to be Mack's specialty: solving the unsolvable with a certain lack of evidence.

In this particular case and instance, she ended up using a "bug" or rather a wire, to find out that several nurses were also victims of the money-slave generation, where, amongst themselves, they admitted to stealing. They stole medicine for money that they would then use to pay underlying debts from the cost of living, student loans, or other forms of expenditures.

Since she needed a warrant for actually pressing charges for their actions, Mack had to wait because the case that she was actually investigating had to do with a doctor. Although, the nurses involved with the stealing did mention the fact that a doctor had some dealings with patients. Mack usually found this information out during the evening so that she could plan how to investigate and the fact that she was sometimes left alone in the evenings. Having a recording of voices helped her not feel quite so alone.

After about a week and a half of this, Mack had the information she needed and the proper documents to put the doctor away. It was morning when she went to the hospital to arrest Dr. Roger Marks. Entering into the office, uninvited, Mack was shocked to discover a crime in progress as the culprit fled into the next room. Unable to pursue due to her advanced condition, she checked for a pulse. After finding none, she called in help and explained the situation. Thankfully for her, there was a very kind and caring nurse who sat her down with a glass of water. As if things couldn't get any worse with a murderer on the loose, Mack felt a pain. This was a pain that she was familiar with because it meant that she was going into labor. Calling Detective Tyler Clarke, she said, "Hi, are you busy?"

"At the moment, no, I'm not. I'm on lunch right now. Why?"

"You might want to clear your schedule and get to the hospital."

"Okay, I'll be right there."

"Thanks. Also, oh, never mind. I'll just see you when you get here."

"Okay, I'll be there as soon as I can." It was about twenty minutes before Tyler arrived at the hospital. By that time, Mack was in a hospital bed and her doctor was in the room with her. As she was getting ready for that, her mind was analyzing the suspect that she had briefly seen. Even though she hadn't seen the face, Mack had seen some other subtleties that would help identify him or her.

It wasn't until after she had a set of twin girls that she recognized the culprit and had Tyler Clarke follow him in order to arrest him. Detective Clarke followed and arrested him, but it wasn't without its disturbances. "Doctor Duncan Davis, you are under arrest for the murder of Doctor Roger Marks."

"I'm being arrested solely by a witness's statement?"

"By the best detective that Fairbanks has ever known."

Detective Clarke read his rights and directly afterwards, with a sneer on his face, he said, "You won't ever see your little girls again." That's when Tyler lost his cool for a second, but he had a friend with him who saved his reputation and his temper.

"Tyler, try to find them and I'll take this guy to the department." The friend said.

"Thanks." Tyler left them and went to find his twin daughters. It was five minutes later when Mack received word that one of her daughters didn't make it. She was shown the other daughter by a nurse: Nurse Val Mor're.

The nurse said, "Ma'am, I had someone try to pay me off to take this precious baby girl of yours to the morgue, but I couldn't do that and I didn't do that."

"Thank you. I really appreciate it. I just hope that I can find my other daughter also, if she's still alive."

"Ma'am, there was another nurse: Carmen Coralez. The man, who approached me, also approached her."

"Thank you."

When Detective Tyler Clarke stopped by the hospital room, Mack informed him of the recent developments, to which, he immediately set off to find Carmen Coralez. When she was found, it wasn't a pretty picture. Carmen had been killed and locked up in a janitor's closet with a note that stated:

'I did it! I stole the baby. Now try to find me instead!'

This made another mystery to solve that was making this problem even more and more intricate and maze-worthy by the moment. This turn of events required Tyler to have the note taken to the lab and the murder documented. Due to the tests that had to be run, the full results wouldn't be available until 1-2 days after it was submitted, sealing the fate of Tyler and Mack's daughter. Unless they had a profound breakthrough, their daughter could be dead, dying, or otherwise in trouble. Needless to say, it was a frustrating 24-48 hours for them.

When the results came in, it eliminated most suspects, providing one: the janitor, Carlos Airez. When Detective

Clarke went to investigate Carlos's residence, the janitor wasn't there. There was fresh tire marks leading off into the woods and he pursued them.

After several different paths and roads, they ended up near Nenana, Alaska. That's when he realized where Carlos was and had been heading towards: the Nenana municipal airport. Tyler arrived there just as a plane lifted off with Carlos Airez and his little baby girl on board. Tyler immediately talked with the airport control and spoke with a reluctant, cantankerous person who insisted that he got a warrant. Either that, or inform the Alaska State Patrol of his plight. If Carlos went into Canada, then they had no chance of pursuing them. If he went down to the Lower 48 then the FBI would have to be informed, making it a federal case.

In the end, he ended up going back to the hospital defeated. Tyler then told Mackenzie, "Mack, I tried to get him, but I wasn't able to do so. What do you suggest? I can't think."

"We should inform the chief of this. If he can't do anything within a month then we'll start our own detective agency. Our family is growing and we need to be there for our sons and daughters. If we have our own business of investigating then we'll be able to have more of a family life."

"All right, I'll let the chief know." He gave her a quick kiss before he left for the Fairbanks Police Department. Entering in, there was the usual activity as if the world knew nothing of the other people in it and their losses. Minor offenders were being filed; people were bailing out that family member or friend who had too much of a good thing, and the usual people were inquiring and filing complaints. Walking to the chief's office and knocking at the door that was already open, he asked, "May I come in, Chief?"

"Sure, go ahead and close the door."

"Thanks." Tyler shut the door and took the seat offered to him.

"Chief, have you heard of any activity lately?

"Yes, but let me just say my congratulations first."

"Thanks, but what have you heard?"

"That there was a flight out of Nenana that was outside of our jurisdiction where a man and a baby took a plane flight out of there. Another person thought that it was suspicious and filed a report. The Nenana police contacted me about it since that person worked as a janitor at the hospital. He's unmarried and hasn't had a serious relationship. They wondered if anyone made a report of an abducted or stolen baby."

"Chief, that baby is mine. Mack had twins and one was stolen. A couple of murders later and that will bring us to our present situation: the suspect flying off. The airport control wouldn't tell me anything so; I was unable to do anything in my current position regarding this matter.

"Well, I can tell you that we'll do everything we can, but we can only do so much."

"I know, Chief. That's why we, meaning Mack and myself, came up with a solution. If you can't find them in one month then we're going to start our own detective agency. That way, we'll have more family time and we can pursue this matter further."

Tyler informed the chief who nodded and said, "That's fair enough, considering your time on the force and your current predicament."

"Thanks, Chief."

"You're welcome."

"I'm going to do some more work then I'm going to call it a day."

"Sounds good, so could you give this to Mack for me?"

"Sure," Tyler said, taking the brown envelope addressed to Senior Detective Mackenzie Murphy Clarke. It wasn't until after work that Tyler was able to take the envelope to Mack.

When she opened it, her expression showed no surprise at its contents: a letter of congratulations and a case file about several complaints made about ineffective morphine with a warrant to be used to arrest the suspected person or persons. "Tyler, I believe you can help me with this. I already have the evidence and the suspects. I just need you to make the arrest tomorrow."

"Okay, do you want to come home now or have you been released yet?"

"I should be released tomorrow. The doctor is concerned about dehydration and stress after what has happened."

"Okay, I love you and I hope that you have a good night." Tyler gave her a kiss goodnight before he left to go home.

It was on his way home that he stopped and talked with a hitchhiker. "Where you headed?"

"I'm heading to the North Pole."

"Well, hop in. I'll give you a lift."

"Thanks." The hitchhiker was a middle-aged man with a plaid shirt and a backpack on his back. He took off the backpack and climbed into the passenger seat. "I've been trying to get a ride to the North Pole for a while now, but I haven't had any luck. I was beginning to think that there were no more good people left in this world."

"I think that myself sometimes. Some people are like that in this life and you just have to deal with them no matter how unsatisfactory those dealings are. Do you have family in the North Pole?"

"No, I have a job there for the summer. I wish I actually lived up here instead of having the wanderer's creed of being footloose and fancy-free."

The man reminded Tyler of someone he knew so he asked, "Where did you grow up at?"

"Oh, I grew up in Idaho mostly. Have you ever heard of Council, Idaho?"

"Yes. Have you ever heard of the detective in Idaho? The famous Detective Matthew Murphy?"

"Sure, I've heard of him. He's an amazing detective who solved some of the unsolvable cases. Why?"

"I've worked with him and you just seemed familiar to me.

"That's crazy. He's related to me since he's my uncle. When did you work with him?"

"I actually worked with him on a couple of occasions. Do you know his daughter?"

"Yes, Mackenzie Murphy?"

"She's my wife so you do have at least one relative up here. In fact, I'll give you my number in case you need it."

"Thanks. Do you know where 132 Santa Claus Lane is?"

"Yes."

"That's where I need to go."

"Okay." Tyler drove the man to his destination and gave him his phone number.

"Thank you."

"You're welcome. Have a great night." Tyler drove off and went home.

Two days later. . .

Tyler had arrested the nurses and had forgotten all about the man he had given a ride to when he received a phone call. "Hello?"

"Hi, is this Tyler?"

"Yes."

"Your number was found on a body and we need to find out what happened. Can you come out to North Pole?"

"Sure, just give me the address." He wrote down the address before he drove to the destination.

Upon arriving at the scene of the crime in his Fairbanks Police Department squad car, the investigator had to do a double-take. "Hi, I'm Caroline Whitmansen. I'm the investigator on this case."

"It's nice to see you again, although, I wish it was under different circumstances. I'm Detective Tyler Clarke. I drove this man to 132 Santa Claus Lane where he said that he had work. That was two days ago. Do you have any leads?"

"You're the only lead that we have so far."

"Where's his pack?"

"He didn't have a pack when we arrived on the scene."

"Okay, we need to find his pack and check with a logging company to see if they're missing a worker or two."

"Why?"

"This man has boots, a plaid shirt, and traces of sawdust on his work pants, so he must be doing some seasonal work. All clues point towards logging or forestry work." Tyler then noticed boot prints leading away into some brush. Following them, Tyler found the man's pack and a note addressed to him. It stated:

"Your daughter is still alive, but you won't ever find her or me again. Don't even try. To try is to fail and fail again."

Tyler gritted his teeth and turned the evidence, including the note, over to Caroline. "Mack had twins and one was stolen away. The person who did this also did that. I want this guy just as bad as you do. Am I still a suspect?"

"No, you've pretty much cleared your own reputation. Let me know if there is anything I can do to help you. I can tell that you're on a quest to find your little girl. Tell Mack hi from me."

"Okay, will do." Tyler left and went back to the department. All the while, he kept wondering about the madness of the man . .

One month later . . .

Tyler and Mackenzie opened the door of their new detective agency. That's when the chief of police stopped by. "Hi, this place looks great, but that's not why I came by. I thought you'd be interested to know that the authorities in Colorado found Carlos Airez. Unfortunately, he was found dead in a ditch with a few bullet wounds. He had to be identified by his dental records and there was nothing else on him. There were no clues as to where your daughter could be. Sorry about this turn of events."

"Thanks, Chief. We appreciate you letting us know."

"You're welcome. It seems as though you've finally found the unsolvable. I'm just sorry that it had to involve your own daughter. What are you two going to do?"

"We're going to continue investigating. There are still criminals and crimes being committed out there. At the end of the day, it is just reassuring to know that one more criminal is put away. It'll never make up for our daughter's disappearance, but it helps to prevent someone else from having the same problem. That or it justifies a wrong by having them pay. This is a job that is bittersweet, yet we love to solve the puzzles of it to create completeness."

"All right, then I'll leave you to your task of the impossible possibilities." The chief left and Mack leaned into Tyler's chest, his arms encompassing her, comforting a mother who had lost a child even though she had gained experience through it all. What Mack couldn't understand was: why didn't this type of thing happen to Sherlock Holmes? Or maybe it had and they just hadn't heard about it. In either case, the fact still remained that there was a case that she was unable to solve. Unfortunately, that was a case that took away one of her own.

Now, emotional determination took over all rational deduction. A tear trickled down her cheek as a steely resolve to ensure that no more families had to deal with the suffering of losing a child in any way, shape or form. Or, if they did, they would at least have some sort of peace knowing that the person who committed the act wouldn't be able to follow through with another malicious and selfish act.

That is the thing which Mackenzie strove for: a world without crime. It was an impossible task that would probably never be completed, but often, it's the challenges we face rather than the impossibility. That's why, at the end of the day, Mack was able to lay down her head and fall asleep. There was still an irrepressible curiosity about where her daughter was and what had happened, but that was the problem about rationality. Emotion was the irrational rational that one would never cease in wondering about those lost or missing.

As she slept, Mack dreamed of all those people she had met in all her cases and of all the people who had suffered the loss of a loved one. A smile, or what could be considered a smile, in her sleep came into play as her dream took her to all the successes she had ever had and all the people that she had put away behind bars that would never strike again, or so she hoped. Still, it was more wins than losses that could make someone into a winner, so Detective Mackenzie Lynn Murphy Clarke had a successful career.

Now, she had another adventure ahead of her: balancing her job as a self-employed detective in their detective agency and motherhood. The dream ended with the closing of a leather-bound journal that had the words: *Chase Dreams, Strive for Adventure* and *Live Like There's No Tomorrow* inscribed upon the cover. Murphy's Law is Mack Murphy's law, concluding the case as a dreamless sleep took over. Even though, there are always more cases to be had, Mack Murphy would solve them in peace without another readers' or writers' imagination to daunt the determined detective. So, I say, or rather write for the last time: Case #32: Doctor Deceit of the Detective Mackenzie Murphy Series is closed.

CASE 32 ACTIVITIES:

CRITICAL THINKING:

What are your thoughts regarding Detective Murphy Clarke? Do you think she had a successful career capturing criminals? If there was to be another series, what do you think that series would be about? In what ways have Mack's techniques regarding detective work changed from the very first case that she was involved with? Has it changed for the better or for the worse? Write a paper about Detective Mackenzie Murphy. What was your favorite case? What was your least favorite case? What would you like to see if there are any future detective series?

BONUS ACTIVITY:

 Submit your thoughts regarding this detective series to the author: clchase32@gmail.com

REVIEW QUESTIONS:

1) What detective techniques does this case involve? Why are they effective or ineffective?

2) What momentous occasion happens during this case? How does this affect the next problematic chain of events?

3) Why does the culprit get away from the detectives? What made this escape possible?

4) What does this case foreshadow about Mack's family and future?

VOCABULARY:

Define and use in a sentence based on the definition for the word.

Subtleties-

_____

_____

Cantankerous-

_____

_____

VOCABULARY REVIEW:

Unscramble the word and write down the word's definition.

nngeius- arising

_____

teipxslo- adventures

_____

lhsseurt- merciless

_____

ABOUT THE AUTHOR

C. L. Chase was born and raised in Idaho, but currently resides in Fairbanks Alaska. The adventures of Detective Mackenzie Murphy are somewhat based on the author's own experiences despite being a work of fiction. C. L. Chase has been involved as a Civil War Re-enactor, an assistant crew leader for a conservation corps, a dog sled handler, and a few other pursuits. Among those pursuits has been the hobby of writing that has made the Detective Mackenzie Murphy Series a reality.

The first book published by C. L. Chase was Detective Mackenzie Murphy Series: Cases 1-16 since this is the continuation of the book. It was also the hobby of writing and publication of her first book that has also led her to become a self-publisher and set up her own business to publish her own books. That self-publishing business is known as: Chase Dreams Publishing. This is done in the hopes that others, like you, might be entertained by the book and be inspired to Chase your own Dreams.

Contact the author by e-mail: clchase32@gmail.com
Or, you can write mail to:
Chase Dreams Publishing
3875 Geist Rd. STE E PMB # 149
Fairbanks AK 99709